Highpockets

Other books by Douglas Savage:

A Mouthful of Dust

The Sons of Grady Rourke

Incident in Mona Passage

Cedar City Rendezvous

The Court Martial of Robert E. Lee

The Glass Lady

Untold History of the Civil War Series:

Women in the Civil War

The Civil War in the West

Civil War Medicine

Ironclads and Blockades in the Civil War

Prison Camps in the Civil War

Rangers, Jayhawkers, and Bushwhackers in the Civil War

The Soldier's Life in the Civil War

Highpockets

A Novel

Douglas Savage

M. EVANS
Lanham • Boulder • New York • Toronto • Plymouth, UK

Published by M. Evans
An imprint of Rowman & Littlefield
4501 Forbes Boulevard, Suite 200, Lanham, Maryland 20706
www.rowman.com

10 Thornbury Road, Plymouth PL6 7PP, United Kingdom

Distributed by NATIONAL BOOK NETWORK

British Library Cataloguing in Publication Information Available

Library of Congress Cataloging-in-Publication Data Available

ISBN 0-87131-757-5 (cloth : alk. paper)
ISBN 978-1-59077-215-7 (pbk. : alk. paper)
ISBN 978-1-59077-216-4 (electronic)

∞™ The paper used in this publication meets the minimum requirements of
American National Standard for Information Sciences—Permanence of Paper
for Printed Library Materials, ANSI/NISO Z39.48-1992.

Printed in the United States of America

For Lizy D.

"My heart's in the highlands,
my heart is not here."
—*Robert Burns*

Chapter One

"YOU THERE, HOLD or I'll open you up!"

Beside a yellow fire, the loud man stood tall and thick as a tree. The flame flashed dully against the six sides of one iron branch pointing into the darkness where a boy stood frozen with blind terror.

"Come closer, or I'll blast you into coyote feed!"

The boy trembled, waiting for the muzzle's explosion. The spreading wetness in his baggy and colorless trousers felt hot in the bitter night chill. A red memory of white men in buffalo coats and with their hands dripping blood drove the warm water from his shaking body.

"I'll not be telling you again." The bull voice spoke slowly, with a severe cadence.

The boy's English was barely adequate for the brevity of the huge man in the fire light. It was time to advance: better to feel the hot lead in the warm light than to perish in the wild and freezing darkness.

The bedraggled boy shuffled toward the raised weapon. A massive fur coat hung from the great man's broad shoulders down into the dust and powder-fine snow. A wide fur hat topped the figure's square and bearded face. The man lowered the browned muzzle until it reached the boy's eye level.

The boy's wide stare followed the six-sided, browned barrel up to the wooden stock where his eyes met one lined and weathered eye nearly shut as it squinted into the heavy musket's rear sighting groove.

Without lowering the shooting iron below the boy's chin, the furclad figure opened both of his eyes. He looked down his rifle into the grave eyes of the haggard boy. Everything about the big man was hard. His right hand gripped the weapon's blackened trigger guard. Deep furrows lined the wide, grim face which remained stuck to the rifle's stock. The boy's terror focused on the old man's eyes.

There was something about the gray eyes of the tall man. They oozed warmth in the icy blackness of the night on the high plains. The old man's eyes were creased with deep lines which reached from their corners back to where the bushy fur hat touched his ears. In the weary eyes, the boy imagined a deep well where a world of sorrow had been dumped. The boy had seen such eyes before.

The boy blew a long sigh born of unspeakable fatigue. In the stunning clarity shining from the old gray eyes, the boy's numbing fear broke like the last of a fever.

With his raised musket, the man motioned for the boy to step sideways to the left as the man took one long stride to his right. Both stood on the same side of the fire where the crackling and sparking of the flames further pacified the boy. The man aimed the muzzle at a fat log ten paces from the fire. The boy followed the musket's aim to the log until he stood with his heels touching the fallen timber.

The man pointed the muzzle at the ground where the log lay. The boy squatted on the cold hardness of the frozen tree. Only the popping of the fire broke the silence absolute.

The boy sat stiffly as the mountain man lowered the rifle after first carefully easing down the rifle's hammer half way to its tiny, percussion cap.

With his big iron's stock braced against his boot which protruded from his man-long, fur coat, the tall man stood at ease with the rifle's browned barrel nestled in his right hand. He looked at the sitting boy who stretched his hands toward the fire to thaw his fingers which stuck naked from the ends of his woolen mittens. The boy closed his eyes to allow his senseless nerves to absorb the warm relief. The old man squinted at the frail, black-eyed child. The boy appeared to be ten or twelve years old with his narrow shoulders stooped and his faced pinched by cold and hunger. When the boy opened his eyes, the starful sky was obscured by the towering man in fur parka.

The old man turned his back to the boy. That silent gesture sucked the remaining fear from the boy's heart. The man heard the boy's exhausted sigh but he did not turn around until he reached a pile of gear at the edge of the darkness. Stooping, the man separated his possessions with a rustling of cloth and the clanking of tinware. He stood up with his left arm covered with a large blanket. He still gripped the heavy shooting iron.

Without a word, the old man laid the heavy blanket of many colors across the tattered knees of the boy sitting on the fallen timber. The boy's thin face flushed as he remembered the wetness in his trousers. The old man quickly looked away from the boy's lap. The boy wrapped the blanket around his shoulders. Behind him, the great blanket touched the hard ground where his log seat met crystalline snow, fine and dry as talc.

Slowly, the boy's senses warmed beside the fire. His crusted nostrils thawed to the wonderful smell of cooking meat. He squinted into the fire toward a spit rigged across the fire. A jackrabbit sizzled impaled on a twig suspended above the flames. The boy licked his cracked lips when the old man pulled off half of the hot meat. When the old man turned, the boy saw that the big man did not carry the musket in his fist. The man laid the steaming meat into the boy's upturned hands.

The boy flung the rabbit toward his gaunt face. Swiftly, he mumbled an incantation foreign to the man's ears before the hot meat disappeared into the boy's tired face. A smile cracked the hard line of the man's whiskered mouth.

The boy licked his fingers while the man glided in and out of the firelight. He stoked the fire with chunks of timber retrieved from the blackness beyond the camp. On his last trip from the night's smooth edge, the old man stooped again at his pile of stores and tossed more brightly colored blankets onto his furclad arm. With the other hand, he pulled the last of the cooked meat from the fire. Carrying the meat on the stick, he handed it to the boy and turned away.

Between the boy's log and the fire, the old man spread two heavy blankets on the frozen ground after first kicking away the light snow cover. He laid two bright blankets on the ground next to his sack of wares.

The man sat down on his blanket. As he pulled another blanket up to his white-bearded chin, he squinted beside the fire toward the sitting boy. He pointed to the other blankets on the ground close to his own.

"You eat. You sleep there," commanded the old man.

The boy ate, and then, curled up inside the thick wool blankets of many colors beside the big man, the boy slept without dreams.

Chapter Two

THE BOY AWOKE with a start and he felt the corners of his mouth crack dryly in the biting cold. He opened his eyes and closed them quickly against the assault of painfully brilliant daylight. Low in the eastern sky, the morning sun of the high plains glared ferociously.

The boy saw the mountain man clad from head to foot in brown furs. He piled tinder onto the firepit dug into the ground. Beside the fire, a coffee pot steamed deliciously. Only the crackle of the fire broke the dawn's dry stillness.

The boy was surprised to see his bundle of worn clothing and his precious books bound with a leather strap lying in the dazzling snow beside his shoulder. He could not recall fetching them from the night. He smiled with relief that his treasures were safe at his side.

The aroma of the coffee roused the boy who sat upright and felt the cold wind bite at his neck. He rubbed his eyes with the bare fingers at the ends of his mittens.

The old man turned toward the boy without rising from beside the fire. Steam rose from the bearded face when he said "Coffee?" in a clear, hard voice. The boy knew that English word and he nodded as he pulled himself from the blanket's snug protection.

The boy took a steaming, tin cup of black coffee from the large hand. The cup felt scalding to the boy's blue fingers.

"Thank you," the boy smiled. He sat on the fallen tree and laid the cup beside him. He reached for the heavy blanket which he wrapped around his narrow shoulders. The colorful blanket was still warm with sleep.

The old man studied the boy and he looked at the four, long white fringes which ran out from under the front and the back corners of the boy's coarse, peasant blouse. Without picking up the cup of cooling coffee, the boy placed his gloved hands on his knees, looked to the snow, and mumbled his strange and soft song. The old man watched the boy rock back and forth in time to his subdued monotone. With eyes closed, the boy thanked the God of his fathers' house for bringing him safely to another day and for the bread from the earth.

The boy closed his eyes to concentrate upon the bitter coffee which soothed him to the bone. He looked over toward the furclad man and nodded. The man of the mountains returned to working his fire.

Far to the east, the orange sun shimmered over white plains. The sun's glare on the sparkling snow was painful to the eye. The boy followed the hazy line of the horizon where it merged gently into the purple sky. Close to the earth, the sky was deep blue, becoming more purple directly above. Looking westward, the boy saw an unbroken range of blue mountains which ran north and south as far as his snow-blind eyes could see. Their peaks were white.

The boy stood and rolled up his blankets as the old man had done. He carried them to the man along with his empty tin cup. Without a word, the man took the cup and the boy's blankets and stuffed them into his bulging sack of stores. Before the boy could turn away, the man reached into his heavy sack and pulled out a large, furry parka like his own. He slipped the fur over the boy's head without disturbing the boy's small-billed, soft hat. The fur cape fell heavily upon the boy's narrow shoulders.

The boy turned and walked back to where his bed had been on the frozen ground of early fall on the high plains.

The boy noticed that his boots made a delicate crackling sound in the new snow. His feet were already numb from the bitter cold. The man took silent note.

Reaching into his canvass sack, the tall man pulled out two, furry tufts. He carried them over the crunchy snow toward the boy.

"Put these on to keep out the cold, boy." The old man gestured toward the boy's freezing feet.

Examining the long furs, the boy saw two wide pelts stitched lengthwise with leather thongs. Seeing them to be similar to the old man's fur leggings, he sat down upon his fallen log which stung his backside with icy hardness. He pulled the hides over his boots and he soon had fur from his toes to his knees.

Under his fur hat, the towering hard face of the man cracked into a smile. Deep furrows creased from the corners of his gray eyes all the way back to the white hair which escaped from the fur hat. When the old man smiled, the boy understood that he would not again fear the powerful figure into whose camp the spirits of the night had led him with wet pants and an empty belly.

"Where you bound, boy?"

The boy rolled the old man's drawling English over his mind which was filled with Russian and with the ancient dialects of his father's house a world away. The boy said nothing.

"Well, boy?" the old man squinted in the harsh sunlight.

Collecting the old man's few words into his mind where he made them over into Russian, the boy raised his mittened hand. He pointed away from the sun toward the western mountains.

"The mountains, boy?"

"Vest," said the boy softly on clouds of steam. "I go vest. . . . That way."

"West, is it? Not likely with winter coming down hard and fast." The old man shook his head. "Not likely."

"Vest," the boy protested grimly.

"Only if you want to feed the bears up there," the old man said pointing with his gray beard toward the far bare peaks. The man studied the boy's hollow cheeks and his sunken eyes.

"If you have a mind to, you can come along with me. That way."

The man raised his huge fist and pointed toward the ridges beneath the low sun in the southeast. "Come spring, you can be on your way."

The boy worked on the words and their kindly tone, foreign to his ears. Thinking of the old man's company and of the terrible march alone toward the western ridges, the boy had two choices: freeze alone or take his chances with the hard stranger who had shared his meat, his fur, and his fire.

In his mind, the boy heard his father's voice. His father was a learned bookman. He remembered his father's favorite story about how Abraham had argued with God, praised be He, to spare the lives of the wicked people in the town of Sodom. The Almighty agreed to save the people only if Abraham could find but ten righteous people there. So his father's kind believed that God spares the whole Earth each new day because somewhere in the world there are always ten people who are without blame. They do not even know that they are one of The Ten for whose sake the world is saved daily from destruction. Perhaps, thought the boy, this old man of few words was one of The Ten?

"That way," the boy said pointing toward the mountains to which the old man had gestured.

The old man looked down into the thin face and he said with a smile, "There you be, Cub."

The boy would come to learn that so long as he stood in the long shadow of this giant of few words, he would be "Cub." Although he had not heard that English word before, he knew that it had a warm sound about it.

As his breath steamed toward the white breath of the child, the big man turned toward the far brown mountains with their white peaks. He trudged off ahead of the boy and he carried his great sack slung across his broad back. Nestled into the crook of his furclad elbow, the long barrel of the heavy Hawken rifle glistened coldly in the bright dawn. The iron's hammer was eared back to the safe, half-cock position, primed to touch off the morning's new load of corned, black powder packed hard behind a lead ball the size of the tip of the boy's thumb.

Two hundred paces from the campsite in the new snow, the boy trotted behind the man into a stand of fir trees. The white clearing disappeared behind them and the tall timbers swallowed the two travellers already weary from the bitter cold. The boy heard the man's words which drifted backward in a cloud of steam.

"Today, Cub, we go high."

Chapter Three

WITHIN THE FOREST of pines, the world had three colors: The lightly packed snow was starch white; the trees were a wall of evergreen firs; and the morning sky was purple.

Four furclad boots moved with snow-muffled thuds in time to the panting of two straining chests. The boy stomped heavily into the old man's tracks as they made their winding way through the dense trees. He could hear no sound save for his labored breathing and his pounding head. Stumbling onward with his head bowed to keep pace with the man's march, the boy tripped and fell often into the new footprints ahead of him. When the boy's body tumbled into the snow, the man neither turned nor stopped.

In his aching thighs burning with fatigue, the boy felt their gradual climb to an unseen summit hidden by the old man and by the tall trees which engulfed them like a cold sea of brittle green smelling faintly of pine tar.

When the man came to an abrupt halt, the boy marched into his backside. The boy's blue lips tasted the cold dampness of the mountain man's fur back before the boy fell backward over his own feet. On his hands and knees, the boy heaved out great clouds of steam as he gulped the freezing air which burned his lungs. He closed his eyes and worked to keep from throwing up into the trapper's boot prints.

As the boy rocked backward to sit upon his heels, the old man laid his baggage into a snow drift and he turned to face the anguished child.

"We rest here."

When the boy, now called Cub, opened his eyes to look up to his tall companion, the boy's face met an outstretched, fur mitten which handed the boy a crisp, black ribbon of dry, jerked meat. The boy's mittened hand trembled from the cold as he pulled the jerky to his nose for a sniff. Sitting cross-legged in the dry snow, the boy nodded his gratitude as he bit off a bite of his tough ration. Behind clenched teeth, he paused to murmur his strange and soft song. With stiff fingers, he fumbled to touch the long, dirty fringes which he could not find beneath his heavy, new parka. Satisfied that the coarse meat was not pork, the boy munched the hard jerky which went down warmly.

The old man took three long strides toward a flat, blackened tree stump where he sat down heavily beside the boy who sat in the fine, powdery snow. With a puff of steam from behind his ice-encrusted beard, the man pointed to another nearby stump. The boy heaved himself upward and sat on the cold stump at the end of the man's furry arm.

As the jerked meat revived him, the boy watched the man who did not eat. Instead, his great white head was erect with closed eyes. Around the hole in his iced beard, steam rose into the bright sunshine which filtered down through the high treetops. The steam rose in clouds which slowly vanished as the old man's breathing became shallower and shallower behind his closed eyes.

Not a leaf nor twig stirred in the morning stillness. Not a trace of wind touched the boy's red cheeks. The quiet was broken only by the muffled impact of a snow clump or pine cone falling to the earth. The snow instantly swallowed the dull sound. The boy could feel the eerie tranquility which lay upon him.

The old man opened his eyes and he rose with one smooth motion. The boy allowed the last bite of the jerky to linger warmly in his mouth as he rose behind his guide. As the boy caught up with the tall man and matched his long strides, he saw a cloud of white steam swirl about the gray and white curls under the man's wide fur hat.

"I am called Highpockets."

Through the forest they trekked leaving a wake of steam from their breath rising among the pillars of daylight which joined the violet sky to the white floor of the forest.

Although the boy was snug inside his fur parka, his exposed face was numb from the cold. His chin dripped ice-water where his warm breath condensed. He gathered the fur collar higher about his neck to cover his freezing face. He was able to work the fur upward to reach his numb nose. As the boy stumbled to keep pace with the old man, he buried his face downward into the parka. Only his eyes braved the biting cold. He blinked often to warm his eyeballs dried by the wind.

The trees seemed to stand aside to reveal a man-wide path which wound through the dense underbrush and towering pines. The path gradually steepened as the boy struggled to put his cold feet into the footprints made by the old man who called himself Highpockets. Whenever the boy lingered too far behind the old trapper, he felt a biting cold breeze which the old man's back had blocked. The boy worked to stay within the warm wake of the mountain man.

When at last the old man stopped, the boy did not walk into him. He was too far behind. Turning, the old man laid his pack upon the snow where he waited for the boy to stumble to him. The boy's face was hidden behind a veil of steam as he watched the tall man dust snow from atop a tree stump before sitting upon its jagged and rotted surface.

The boy sat down hard on a nearby stump. He closed his eyes against the pain of the cold.

The mountain man handed jerky to the boy who could not raise his mitten to receive it. The boy's hand dropped limply to his side. His brain spun from the cold and from dizzying weakness down to his bones. He did not feel the big trapper's powerful arm braced behind him as he nearly rolled backward into the new snow. He breathed in convulsive pants and the searing cold burned his throat. The boy longed to hold his breath so his mouth might warm and moisten. But he could not stop panting which burned all the way down to his heart.

Highpockets lifted a canteen to the boy's cracked lips. The boy allowed the cool water to drip down his throat as he rested against the long, hard arm. Because the old man carried his canteen under his parka to prevent it from freezing, the water felt comfortable to the boy.

"The water will bring you around, Cub," Highpockets said softly.

The trapper removed his arm when he felt the boy's back tighten and his vigor return.

The boy wrapped his chapped lips around the English "Thank you."

"You are doing fine, boy. The strength will come soon enough.

The old man pointed to the jerky which stuck stiffly from the boy's mittened hand. Closing his eyes for his mysterious incantation, the boy smiled weakly and he lifted the meat to his face. Then Highpockets raised a piece of dried, black meat and waved it at the chewing boy.

"Jerky," Highpockets said.

"Jerky," the boy replied with his thick accent.

"Jerky," the trapper repeated as he snapped off another bite with his perfect teeth.

The boy pointed to the canteen slung over Highpockets' chest.

"Canteen," the old man instructed.

Highpockets shook the canteen. "Water," he said.

"Voda," the boy replied. The big man smiled.

The mountain man opened his furry parka long enough to sling the canteen over his shoulder inside the great coat. He picked up his heavy pack and musket which had been propped against his tree stump. The smaller bundle he handed to the boy.

"What year is it, boy?"

Cub seemed puzzled. The calendar of his father's house which marked a dozen festivals and holidays went back five centuries. But he knew what Highpockets meant.

"1855."

"Oh? Then who's president of the country now?" The man seemed somehow surprised by the boy's answer. Perhaps he had not thought of time or of the world beyond the mountains for many seasons.

The boy worked hard in a far place called New York to learn about this strange and wonderful place called America. He concentrated to make his numb lips make the English sounds of a name.

"Franklin Pierce. He is presidentum."

"My God!" Highpockets laughed. "General Pierce? I soldiered with him in Mexico, in '47. I'll be damned."

The tall man chuckled for a moment before the hard determination returned to his face.

Looming above the boy he called Cub, Highpockets slowly turned full around in his tracks, making one complete circle. He did not leave the spot in the snow where he stood; he simply turned around. The old man surveyed the forest surrounding them.

The boy studied the deep lines around the clear, gray eyes where Highpockets squinted against the fierce daylight glaring off the snow. When the old man pushed slowly into the trees, the boy followed. When the boy looked behind him as they walked, he was surprised that he could not pick out their resting place of moments ago. Their world was without landmarks: only white earth, brown and green trees, and the purple sky above. Turning toward the trapper's furry back, the boy could not feel lost.

They marched for an hour. Part of their course followed a clearly defined trail, wide enough for two men to walk side by side. The next stretch snaked between the trees, each looking precisely like the next to the boy.

The brilliant sun had fallen below the green treetops to their right leaving behind a veil of gray. The whiteness of the snow and the green wall of fir trees deprived the boy's senses of the texture of the living world. He welcomed upon his red face the sting of the cold air. It was comforting to feel anything in the deathly quiet treescape which had no sound, no real color, and no smell to his numb nostrils.

The boy forced his rubbery legs to plow onward toward Highpockets, lest he fall too far behind and disappear forever.

Chapter Four

ONCE THE SUN vanished behind the western wall of evergreens, the forest absorbed all shadows. Even with the clear sky still coldly blue, the woods were already gray.

In the deepening and silent gloom between the trees, Highpockets stopped his dogged march. He made his slow turnabout through a complete circle. After pointing toward a small clearing within the tall firs, the trapper led the boy to a small open area of fallen timbers.

Highpockets set his sack of stores atop a short, flat stump and he gestured for the boy to do likewise. The old man laid his heavy Hawken rifle against the stump.

Turning his back to Highpockets, the boy looked over his shoulder along their wearisome path. He saw that it was not a trail at all, but only dirty footprints which disappeared among the trees.

By the time the boy balanced his bundled books and ragged clothing upon a stump half-buried in snow, Highpockets had cleared the snow from a small circle on the ground. With his boot, the old man shovelled the snow sideways until he reached brown, frozen earth. Highpockets piled broken branches and armloads of small logs upon the cleared area three feet across.

Slumped atop his cold stump, the boy wanted to help Highpockets who had not yet rested after their day-long effort. But his numb body would not move. So he closed his dry eyelids and he tucked his hands under his furclad arms to thaw his fingers.

The boy did not stir until he heard the snap of Highpockets' wedge of flint striking the trapper's long knife at the edge of the pile of tinder. He opened his eyes in the dusky grayness to see Highpockets kneeling and blowing gently into his bare, cupped hands which protected tiny sparks from the chill breeze. The old man nursed his fragile spiral of smoke. As the small flame spread beneath the stacked kindling, Highpockets rocked back upon his knees and raised his hands over the smoking pile. As the fire crackled and spread, Highpockets with closed eyes waited its comfort. Sitting on his tree stump, the boy stretched his tattered mittens toward the flames.

The boy studied the quiet mountain man who sat with his eyes lightly closed beside his new fire. The old face betrayed a weary tranquility. Such a face reminded the boy of the many faces he had left behind in a squalid village on the far side of the world. This old man's furrowed face radiated that peculiar resignation of the heart which shined like a light from the faces of the village—the *shtettle*—where the boy had been raised. The feeling gave the boy a strange sense of kinship with the old man as weathered as his mountains.

Highpockets stood and reached for his pack. From it he pulled the blankets and the coffee pot. Into the metal pot Highpockets packed clean snow and a single palmful of coffee. He laid the pot at a corner of the blazing fire.

The boy watched the old man clear away a wide patch of snow and underbrush. Turning from the fire, Highpockets walked about their tiny campsite and kicked snow away. Each time his furry leggings revealed a fist-size rock beneath the snow, he picked up the stone and laid it at the base of the flames not quite in the fire. The boy dismounted from his stump to join the old man in his silent search for little stones. The boy kicked the fresh snow until he had deposited a dozen good rocks at the fire's edge. Highpockets and the boy knelt beside the fire.

"Good," Highpockets nodded. "This will do, Cub."

"This will do," the boy repeated with difficulty caused as much by his numb face as by the strangeness of the language after only two years in America.

As silent darkness settled upon the small camp, Highpockets handed the boy a ribbon of hard jerky and a tin cup of hot coffee. Atop his low, hard stump, the boy closed his eyes, raised his gaunt face toward heaven, and softly sang his peculiar blessing. He rocked back and forth.

Highpockets listened. In his youth, the old man learned fur trapping and trading in the grim Yukon territory where the mighty grizzlies fattened themselves on the fur-trapping white men. There, within the Russian camps and posts, he had known many Russian trappers. The boy's words sounded like the language Highpockets remembered from those long-gone camp fires. Highpockets had known a German trader once in the same frozen wasteland. Some of the boy's words also sounded like that German. Highpockets remembered the day he found the German's white bones tied to a tree.

The boy devoured the jerked meat and the hot coffee.

Before Cub finished eating, the forest was black. Only the trees close to the campsite were illuminated by the fire which crackled in the perfect stillness.

The old man stood. Where he had cleared the ground a few paces from the fire, he began digging shallow furrows into the hard earth. He used a hardy sapling pulled from the undergrowth as his shovel to dig trenches in the pattern of two blankets laid side by side. When he finished and exhaled a long gush of steam, he retrieved an armload of the hot stones from the fire's edge. He laid the steaming rocks close together within the furrows. The stones hissed as they touched the frozen ground. Over them, he spread dead brush collected from the forest floor. When all of the stones were covered by a thick layer of brush, Highpockets flung open two of the brightly colored blankets which settled over the warm mound of dry growth atop hot stones.

With puffing effort, Highpockets pulled off his furry leggings. He then stoked the fire with new, dry timber.

Returning to one of the two blankets spread on the ground, Highpockets stretched his long body upon the blanket furthest from the fire. Wearing his parka and his fur hat, he pulled a second blanket up to his white beard.

"Rest well, boy," the old man sighed before closing his wind-burned eyes.

Laying his cup aside, the boy stepped toward the man on the ground. Lying upon his own blanket, Cub pulled a second blanket up to his nose.

The boy lay fully awake between the fire and the old man in the silent darkness of the forest's floor. Through the tree tops, he could see a narrow piece of a brilliant dome of stars which did not twinkle in the frozen, still air. Laying so close to the old man, the boy felt odd. The big man of the mountains was a total stranger to the boy whose short life had been a continuous lesson in finding refuge from the world which despised his father's house, and him, for reasons he could not understand.

But laying there in the stillness broken by the crackling of the fire and the rhythm of the old trapper's breathing, the boy felt kinship with the mountain man sleeping at his side.

The boy felt warm and comfortable. The heat from the stones beneath his bed seeped upward into his exhausted bones. He struggled to keep his eyes open. He wanted to think longer about his march through miles of snowy desolation among towering evergreen pines.

Softly, the boy worked his lips to say "Coffee . . . jerky . . . Highpockets." He tried in a whisper to assume the old man's drawling speech. But the fire sputtering at his side and the warmth rising from the earth and the comfort of the old man's company were too much.

Chapter Five

THE BOY BOLTED upright at the grasp of the old man's hand on his shoulder.

The world was gray as the boy forced his cold eyeballs to focus in the dawn twilight. He shivered beside what remained of the faintly red embers of the fire. Highpockets blocked out the sky still alight with faint stars in the west. The east was barely pink. Highpockets cradled his heavy rifle in his arm as he pulled the boy bodily from his stupor.

"We go, boy," Highpockets commanded. He jerked the boy's blankets from the ground. The boy stumbled backward when Highpockets pushed the boy's bundled stack of books and clothing into the boy's chest.

With his eyes closed against an icy wind, the boy pulled on his furry leggings as Highpockets waited anxiously.

"Come, boy," the big man demanded as he lifted the boy to his feet.

The new sky was pink with daybreak in the high country as the pair moved between the pine trees. Struggling and coughing with exhaustion, the boy pushed himself through the forest, dodging trees and deadfall. In pain, the boy whimpered to himself as he endured the pounding inside his head.

They trotted quickly through the forest for an excruciating hour as the sun climbed in its blue sky between the treetops.

Without a word, Highpockets stopped twenty paces ahead of the boy. The old man's wind came to him in great billows of steam and painful gulps of thin, icy air. The boy collapsed to his knees at the old man's side. Their course had been steepening with each step. Both climbers were exhausted. Highpockets stood gasping with his massive Hawken iron at the ready in his furry mittens.

With the boy slumped at his feet, Highpockets squinted into the forest surrounding them. When he moved, the boy raised his face to watch the old man. The boy squatted in wet snow near the crest of a small hill above a shallow pass full of trees. Highpockets slowly moved down the slippery hillside toward a narrow clearing. Halfway down the hill, the old man stopped. The boy heard the hammer of the Hawken snap back to the full-cocked position. Highpockets raised the browned iron to his right shoulder and he laid his bearded face upon the stock. Behind him, the boy held his breath.

Somewhere behind the boy, a squirrel cackled long and loud. The animal's clucking broke the stillness.

Highpockets raised his furcapped head from the musket. When he eared the iron's hammer down into its safe half-cock, the metallic clicking of the tumblers echoed down the hillside. The tall man lowered the rifle to his side and he rested the butt upon his right boot to protect the polished stock from the snow. He gripped the piece by its browned muzzle and he stood at parade-rest.

After shaking the snow from his legs, the boy stumbled down the hillside toward the trapper. Not until he had reached Highpockets' side could the boy look fully across the pass to the far snowy side.

The divide in the forest might have been a frozen riverbed beneath a blanket of snow. The boy squinted in the sunshine toward the far side and the crest of the opposite hillside.

In the old man's company, the boy had put aside the coppery taste of fear. He tasted it again.

Across the white clearing, at eye-level, the boy saw an Indian warrior astride a beautiful horse. Horse and rider stood motionless amid the towering trees. A long rifle rested upon the animal's neck in the lap of the dark-faced rider.

The dark, mounted man spoke first in his own language, foreign and guttural to the boy's ear. Highpockets responded in the same tongue.

"You are the one called Highpockets?" steamed the rider.

"And you," Highpockets nodded, "are the one called Painted Elk—the law giver."

"I am the law giver. . . . I knew the winter snows would bring you. My council said you would not come. But I, Painted Elk, knew that the one called Highpockets would come as surely as the snow follows the leaves of many colors. Hear me: No harm shall come to you in these my mountains. You shall pass freely as the red-winged hawks. And when the long days bring the new green, you shall come to my council. My young men said that you would not come. . . . But I knew."

The mounted man's words ended in a cloud of steam. His face showed no emotion, only the hardness of sixty winters in the high country.

The boy looked up at Highpockets who stood quietly. The tall man's face was harder than the boy had seen it. Highpockets looked at the dark man and he spoke in his harsh tongue.

"I have heard the words of Painted Elk, the law giver. When the green comes to the hills and the water to the rivers of the high places, I shall come to the council of Painted Elk."

The dark man nodded. He tugged at the reins of his restless pony. Horse and rider turned their backs to Highpockets and the boy. The boy wondered if the old man would raise his rifle. But before the boy could find his throat, Highpockets cradled the iron in his arm and turned toward the hillside. The boy followed behind the mountain man who made his way over the crest of the hill toward their path abandoned before the strange and terrifying meeting deep in the forest.

"This way, Cub," the old man said as they reached their own footprints in the snow. Highpockets did not press on so quickly into the steepening mountains. He moved with long, slow strides between the fir trees.

The white sun climbed above the green firs as the pair marched higher. An occasional break in the wall of pines revealed distant mountain ranges against purple sky. The peaks held the boy's attention whenever they emerged between the trees.

To the boy's eyes after hours of tramping through powdery snow, the far peaks were no longer identical. Each distant ridge took on its own character. Some were shear, rock escarpments. Others were softly rounded with dense green.

In time, Highpockets stopped. The old man made his circle-in-place to survey their position. Ten paces behind, the boy stopped and panted.

Without a word, Highpockets raised his free hand and traced a complete circle across the sky as he slowly turned upon his heels in a little clearing. With snow-blind eyes, the boy followed the old man's mitten.

The boy watched the old man's hand as it waved first toward the purple sky, then across the distant, snowy peaks, then past the green timberline all around them. Highpockets lowered his furry arm to his side. He had said nothing. The boy was silenced by the old trapper's ritual.

Highpockets turned his face toward the boy at his side. The furrowed, bearded face was incandescent in the sunlight. His features radiated a weary peacefulness. Shifting the weight of his heavy rifle from one arm to the crook of the other, he led the boy back into the dense tree-stand.

By day's end, the boy could not remember his lonesome days in the wilderness before meeting the man of the mountains who called himself Highpockets.

The man moved through long shadows where he panted, stooped to stoke their fire, and made two beds atop smouldering stones at a new campsite. With the trees all around blocking out the night winds, the boy chanted his mystery, ate, and climbed into his bed of many colors which was warmed by hot stones against hard earth.

Before the boy could even arrange his thoughts, it was morning of another crystal cold day.

Chapter Six

AND SO IT was for many days. Each day, like the last, dawned with bitter cold before another cruel march among the trees.

Higher and higher they climbed with Highpockets carrying his world slung across his back, his ready iron across his arm, and the stumbling boy in his wake of steam.

If the steady climb was strengthening the boy's legs and heart, that progress was erased by the ever thinning air of the mountains.

The boy marked days by labor spent and by his growing English vocabulary fed by the old man's sparse words. Although the days passed slowly and painfully, the cold monotony was broken for the boy whenever the purple sky filled with clouds. On such days, the boy marveled at the many faces of the billowing formations which rolled ponderously between the peaks. The boy came to expect the flat, rounded clouds which ride the crests of the wind whistling over the mountains. He watched for these lens-shaped clouds which grow only above the downwind side of the peaks around them.

When the sky dumped heavy snow, Cub welcomed it for slowing the big man's pace. On a grand and clear day between two days of blizzard which marooned the two beneath their blankets, the boy had time to observe a gradual change in the face of the endless forest.

They had been walking through less and less of the towering, red-barked Ponderosa pines whose faded needles cushioned the floor of the forest. In their place, stands of Douglas firs grew with short and prickly needles.

After more days of following Highpockets ever higher, the forest grew more dense as the firs gave way to tall spruce trees with their thin and pointed tops. The texture of the forest changed almost daily.

Highpockets' few words which drifted back toward the boy on clouds of steam were rich with wonderful sounds when the old man would name this tree or that fleeing animal in its ancient Algonquin Indian tongue. The boy enjoyed rolling the name "wapiti" over his tongue when Highpockets pointed to a huge elk on a distant ridge.

On a windy, gray day, Highpockets and the boy stopped and laid their belongings on two stumps.

"We stop here, Cub." Highpockets made a small clearing in the dry snow. "It is time to make meat." The man laid his shooting iron into the crook of his arm. "Come, boy."

They did not climb far beyond the site of their new camp. Halfway to the crest of a densely forested slope, Highpockets motioned the boy to hunch down at the base of an ancient spruce. The boy squatted in the snow on soft pine needles.

"Wait and be still, Cub."

Highpockets walked toward the top of the rise. He was careful to keep the wind in his face. Reaching the crest surrounded by trees, Highpockets made his slow circle as he studied his narrow world of green and white.

Satisfied that the icy wind blew into his face, Highpockets crouched down at the top of his hill. With his back to the boy who watched from down the slope, the old man surveyed the far side of the hill where it fell away toward a narrow pass between a steep rise two hundred paces distant.

The boy rubbed his cold hands together. He held his breath until he had to let it out with a long cloud of steam.

Then he filled his lungs again of the cold, dry air, over and over in the calm.

The high, thin air muffled all sound except the wind which blew over Highpockets toward the boy.

The old hunter did not stir. Only his eyes moved up and down the gorge before him.

The boy jumped when the world exploded with a rolling and thunderous roar. He looked toward Highpockets who was lost in cloud of white smoke. The stench of burning sulphur reached the boy's numb nose and he blinked at the sickly, bitter taste in the air.

"Come, boy!" Highpockets boomed from the crest of his smoky knoll.

The boy ran into the wind and he stopped beside the old man.

Highpockets had propped the iron against a fir where he knelt beside the antlers of a small deer. Behind the animal's shoulder, a small hole oozed dark blood. The boy swallowed hard.

As Highpockets drew his long knife, the boy stepped back from the kill.

"Cub," the hunter said softly, "the forest has given us life."

Although he could not make out all of the big man's English, the boy took the old man's sad face and his quiet words as a prayer of thanksgiving, equal in dignity to what the boy mumbled under his breath in his father's tongue. The hunter waited until the boy finished before he rolled the deer over onto its back. Then Highpockets pulled a long knife from under his parka and cut a shallow incision from the animal's belly, through its breastbone, up to its throat.

Before the boy could sway with disgust laced with bone-deep hunger, the tall man rolled the deer over onto its gaping wound to allow the innards to fall into the red snow which steamed as the hot life spilled out.

Highpockets stood, panting clouds of steam. He stepped to his heavy Hawken and laid the rifle across the boy's arms.

The boy's knees buckled at the unexpected weight of the ten-pound iron. The boy felt proud of his new treasure.

With a moan, the man heaved the gutted deer over his back.

The boy trudged up the snowy slope behind Highpockets, past the puddle of wet snow where the old man had watched and waited. With the shooting iron cradled in the crook of his arm, the boy took the slippery hill briskly. The Hawken felt strangely light in his arms.

Chapter Seven

THE BOY ARRIVED ahead of the old man at their piles of baggage. He propped the iron against a tree as he had seen Highpockets do it.

When the old man arrived at camp, he knelt down on one knee to ease the deer carcass from his shoulders. He grunted with relief as the animal rolled heavily into the snow.

Overhead, the gray sky darkened where night comes quickly to the high country.

Highpockets returned panting to his feet. He smiled behind his ice-encrusted beard when he saw the boy stacking firewood within a small circle of earth from which the boy had first kicked away the foot-deep snow. Beneath the tall spruces, Highpockets watched the boy move swiftly in search of kindling and round stones to be warmed beside the fire for their beds.

"You did well this day, Cub," Highpockets puffed.

The boy did not have to know all of the English words; he could feel them.

While the boy worked at striking flint to steel at his pile of twigs, the old man knelt beside the slain deer. With flicking strokes of his blade, the mountain man peeled the hide from the pink muscle and winter fat beneath. He hacked at the meat with an iron tomahawk fetched from his coarse sack. By the time the boy had his fire going, the trapper had skinned and quartered the little buck. He had taken care to wrap each chunk of fresh meat in pieces of cloth.

On his knees, the trapper spread the hairy side of the deer hide upon the snow. Opening a little bag secured with a string, Highpockets pulled out a fistful of rock salt which he rubbed into the pink side of the skin. He splashed two more fists of salt into the pelt where he rubbed it hard into the wet hide. When the last of the salt disappeared into the skin, the old man folded the hide into a tight roll, fursideout, which he tied with leather straps.

"That should do till we get home," the old man said.

Stoking his new fire, the boy looked through the smoke. His face looked puzzled. He knew the word "home" and it stuck to his mind.

As the sky became night, the pair sat facing each other on fallen timbers. After the boy finished his grace, the two weary travelers reached eagerly for the deer steaks sizzling upon the fire.

By the time Highpockets and the boy had laid their firewarmed rocks on the frozen earth, the sky was black in starless chill. Laying on his back atop the warm blanket heated from below, the boy was glad to have the big man's warmth beside him. When he edged closer to the old man's furclad body, Highpockets did not protest.

The boy lay awake while the old man dozed at his side. His mind returned to someplace Highpockets called "home." The very word made the boy's groggy head become a jumble of warm smells, familiar voices, and delicious tastes. He closed his eyes as his head rang with the deep voice of his father—a gentle man of many books from whose pages the Almighty spoke. He could feel his heart warmed by the face of his mother, illuminated by the flame from her precious candlesticks upon a white tablecloth reserved for the weekly Princess of Days. From the treasure of his memories, the boy took comfort.

Cub longed to stay awake by the fire. He tried to guess what home called to Highpockets through these forested mountains. He had not imagined that the solitary, old man of the high country might have kin other than what he carried in his tattered sack. The boy's many questions came slower and slower beside the crackling fire.

"Up you be, Cub," sang Highpockets as the boy opened his eyes to the purple sky.

The boy stumbled to his feet in the daylight streaming down through the fir and Aspen trees. The smell of brewing coffee revived him. Shivering as he forced his feet into his frozen boots, the boy lost his balance and fell backward into wet snow. He squinted up at the laughter of the old man.

Highpockets threw his head back and he roared to the sky. The boy was warmed by the sight of the old man's sad face convulsed with laughter. The boy was airborne when Highpockets hoisted him to his feet.

"A fine mountain man you are, Cub."

"A fine mountain man, I am," laughed the boy as he steadied his footing and straightened his fur parka with its four, dirty fringes dangling beneath.

In the old man's silence, the boy thanked his father's God for bringing him and Highpockets to another day.

They broke camp with precision: Highpockets stuffing blankets and tin cups into his sack while the boy poured melted snow from the coffeepot into four canteens. As the boy spread the fire's coals across the ground and doused them with piles of wet snow, Highpockets shouldered his sack full of wares and deer meat. The old man cradled the Hawken iron after first sending a fresh powder charge and round ball down the brown barrel.

The boy fell into step behind the old man walking toward dense firs. The pointed evergreens with their drooping branches heavy with snow passed swiftly this brilliant morning. Their boots made no sound in the wet snow and moulding pine needles.

They picked their way for many hours through new snow which showed an occasional trail of hoof prints from mule deer heading to the lowlands for winter.

Although panting from their march, the boy's legs told him that their steep climb of the last days had shallowed and that their trek covered gentler, tree-lined hills. In breaks within the treetops, the boy was blinded by the sun which felt warm upon his cold face. Highpockets pounded onward ahead of the boy who followed with his face in clouds of steam exhaled by the mountain man.

By mid-day, they hiked across densely forested, flat land for the first time since their first day together. They climbed no longer.

Rounding a towering pine tree, the boy watched the old man stop far ahead. Then Highpockets took one long step forward into a splash of daylight.

The boy followed through the last of the ancient trees looming between himself and the old man.

Cub raised one mittened hand to his face to shield his eyes from the searing sunshine as he reached the old man's side.

With one eye tightly closed behind his raised hand, Cub followed Highpockets. He stepped from the edge of the weeks-deep forest into fierce daylight as if stepping through a green curtain onto a blinding stage.

Chapter Eight

CUB DROPPED HIS bundle into the snow as he stood at High-pockets' side in the sunshine.

With the forest at his back close enough to be felt, Cub joined the mountain man who studied the great plain of snow. Beneath the clear and violet sky, the boy could see blue mountain ridges in the distance. Between the far mountains and his footprints at the edge of the dense forest, the frozen tundra stretched to the far horizon of hazy peaks.

Cub blinked up at Highpockets who stood before the breathtaking plain. They stood side by side in silence for many minutes until the boy could catch his breath in the thin air of the mountain country.

Highpockets pointed his furclad arm toward the far blue hills.

"There, Cub. . . . It is called My Mountain," Highpockets said as he pointed. The boy turned his face from the horizon to look up into the old man's battered face. The old gray eyes glistened beneath white eyebrows. For a long time, the boy studied the face.

Highpockets shouldered his pack and started out across the knee-deep snow. He did not hurry. Had the boy not slowed his own pace, he would have been leading the old man to the place called My Mountain. *My* Mountain was how the tall man said it.

The boy glanced backward over his shoulder to enjoy the sight of the forest retreating. A cold wind blew into their faces and the boy pulled his parka up to his nose and his fur hat down over his eyes. He walked hiding inside his parka until the afternoon shadows lengthened.

As the sun touched the treetops five miles behind them, Highpockets kicked the snow from a bit of ground where he laid his pack. The boy did likewise beside him.

There were neither trees nor hills to break the icy wind which chilled the boy to the bone. Before stooping in the snow to make a shallow firepit, Highpockets reached into his pack and pulled out the colored blankets. He handed two of them to the boy and he kept two. With one of the blankets wrapped around his shoulders, the boy shivered in the cold dusk. Looking skyward, he saw a few faint stars opposite the white sun which touched the far green forest.

From his sack, Highpockets retrieved an armload of firewood which the boy had not seen him gather within the forest.

The old man worked fast to kindle a small fire inside the little walls of snow which he had packed around his pile of twigs. Sitting in the wet snow, Highpockets gave the boy ribbons of hard jerky and they drank cold water from the canteens. The wind across the plain stung their necks.

Highpockets rose, pulled more sticks from his pack, and fed the fire. He returned to the boy but this time he sat with his face into the wind. Through tears brought to his eyes by the bitter wind, the old man peered into the blackness toward My Mountain. The crackling of the fire and the boy's teeth chattering from cold made the only sounds.

Rising after a while, Highpockets used his feet and his hands to build a nest of snow around himself, the boy, and the fire.

Sitting beside the boy, the old man opened wide his colored blanket.

"Here, Cub," the old man said. The boy eased over toward Highpockets and the open blanket around the big man's shoulders. Wrapped inside his own blanket, Cub nuzzled into the old man's parka and his open blanket. When the boy found his niche, Highpockets lowered his blanket around the boy and himself. The boy buried his face into the old man's chest. He felt Highpockets fold his arms around him.

"There you be, Cub." The boy snuggled into the old man's lap. He could taste the wet, furry parka smelling faintly of pine. The big man's breath blew warmly over the boy's hair.

The boy felt warm. He could feel Highpockets' chest rise and fall against his face. Beneath his blankets, he could no longer hear the terrible, night wind.

When the boy felt Highpockets stir and relax the grip of his powerful arms about the boy's shoulders, the boy squirmed and poked his face outside the heavy blanket. He blinked at another morning.

The boy's dry mouth croaked "Good morning, Highpockets," to which the old man nodded, "And to you, Cub."

Highpockets rose, leaving the blankets wrapped around the boy who stood up beneath gray sky heavy with clouds.

Stuffing the blankets into his sack, Highpockets handed the boy his morning ration of jerked venison, chewy as old leather.

The far blue place called My Mountain was lost in haze. The frigid air was calm under wet-looking clouds as the boy fell into step with the trapper who plodded through the snow of the great plain.

After many hours, the old man paused long enough to share a strip of jerky and an icy swallow of water. When the boy had stepped out of the forest onto the plain, he had welcomed the open wilderness. But now he trudged across the desert of snow and he longed for the forest's subtle shadows and its shafts of light filtering through the green treetops.

Their second night since leaving the protection of the trees brought no peace. On the plain, there was no shelter from the mountain winds. Even nestled within the old man's blanket close to Highpockets' warm body, the boy could find no refuge from the cold. The boy could feel that the old man was not yet sleeping in the long winter's night.

"Is it far, Highpockets?" whispered the boy inside the heavy blanket.

"Not far from here, Cub. My Mountain will be waiting for us."

To the boy, it felt as if Highpockets had more to say. He waited patiently as long as he could until the darkness turned the faintest pink in the eastern sky.

With another overcast daybreak, the pair broke camp and struck out across the featureless sea of snow.

At the end of another day, the boy listlessly helped the old man carve their tiny bunker in the snow. Their small fire could not beat back the nighttime cold.

Snuggling up to the old man under their blankets, Cub listened to a cruel wind.

"Tomorrow, boy," the old man whispered. But Cub could not hear and he did not feel the big man's strong arm behind his head.

Chapter Nine

WHEN THE OLD man stirred, Cub opened his eyes to a magnificent sun low in the southeast sky.

Cub looked up to Highpockets who had risen to stand beside the pile of blankets and tinware. The boy could feel the closeness of the far ridges in the clear air. He squinted at the old man.

"My Mountain, Cub," the trapper said slowly in a cloud of steam. He stood there with the sun glaring into his face as the long shadow of My Mountain stretched across the snow.

After his morning blessing and a strip of rubbery jerky, Cub gathered his bundles. Then he and the old man walked into the mountain's long shadow. Highpockets walked briskly to keep pace with the boy who raced toward the breech in the towering ridges.

The boy could see that these mountains, one of which was My Mountain, were very green in the surrounding snowscape. He did not look back over his shoulder. Not seeing the terrible snow plain made it disappear behind him all the faster.

"That way, boy," Highpockets called ahead. The old man pointed toward a path among the pointed trees leading upward along a hillside.

"Easy, Cub." It was the old man's turn to labor to keep pace. Cub led the way along the rising trail broken by back-and-forth switchbacks carved through the trees to ease the

suddenly steep climb. He wondered who had cut this path
between the tall trees.

All day long, Highpockets worked to keep up with the
boy who carried his baggage with the sureness of his youth.
As their shadows faded in the stillness of the winter woods,
the old man reached the boy's side. In the icy, thin air, they
paused to catch their wind. After a moment of peace among
the pines, Highpockets set the pace slowly as they approached
the crest of a rise.

At the top of the steep slope, the old man stopped. When
the panting boy reached his side, they stood together before
a wide clearing. Ahead of them was a splash of sunlight
which filtered through the treetops from behind them.

Under the weight of his great sack, Highpockets stood
silently with his shoulders stooped. He rested the brown
stock of the heavy Hawken musket upon his right boot and
he held the brown muzzle in his mittened, right hand. The
iron pointed toward the purple sky in the direction of the
clearing.

Cub held his breath with wonder as his snow-blind eyes
blinked at a large, log cabin. Glass windows reflected the
setting sun like perfectly square mirrors beside a fire.

He looked up at the old man who did not speak. Cub's
dazzled eyes sought reassurance that he did not stand before
a mirage born of snow blindness or fatigue or the thin air of
the high country.

Highpockets eased his pack from his shoulders to the snow.

"My Mountain, boy. . . . My Mountain."

Cub could only nod with his mouth open.

Eagerly, the boy took one step in the failing daylight toward
the cabin. But Highpockets checked him with his arm.

"Not yet, Cub. This way."

Highpockets descended the last steps down the snowy
path toward the cabin in the clearing. Cub followed silently
as the old man walked all the way around the cabin. They
studied the outside walls.

The old man turned the corner and advanced into the shade along the eastern face of the cabin. Cub saw a covered porch which ran the length of the cabin. This was the front with one wooden door hewn from flat timber planks.

Highpockets took the five steps to the porch. Without stepping foot on the landing, the trapper laid his sack on the porch. Then he turned to the boy, reached for his bundle, and laid it next to his own. He propped the .50 caliber Hawken against the porch wall.

As Cub stood shivering in the cold dusk, Highpockets stood quietly in the last of the long day's sunshine. The sun light shown orange on the pointed roof and the high, stone chimney. The wooden eaves of the gabled roof jutted from beneath deep snow.

"Highpockets? We go in now?" Cub was breathless.

Without turning from his examination of the cabin, the old man quietly said "Tomorrow."

For months, they had climbed miles into the violet sky through ice and blizzard. Cub stood stunned with disappointment.

"Tomorrow, Cub. . . . Sit." The old man stepped behind the boy and cleared snow from atop a tree stump. His mitten uncovered many deep creases in the squat stump marking it as a chopping block.

Cub sat disgusted.

Highpockets walked into the grayness of the porch's shadow. He returned with both sacks but not with the shooting iron. Cub knew that there were still no footprints on the porch—so close and yet so far.

The old man cleared a hole in the snow by the corner of the cabin faintly illuminated by daylight. Cub could not watch the trapper gathering firewood from a wood pile standing against the tight, little house.

The boy did not rise from his cold stump until Highpockets had his firepit blazing close to the boy's feet. As he stretched his hands toward the fire, the flames crackled and warmed his face but not his spirits.

"We have time, Cub." Highpockets' face hardened for an instant. "You need to learn waiting, boy."

The boy struggled to hate the old trapper. But he failed when he looked up into the weary face of Highpockets who knelt beside the fire. The boy rocked backward on his tree stump and lifted his wet, furry boots out of the snow. He pointed his feet toward the fire.

By darkness, they had eaten of the mule deer from Highpockets' pack. Cub was revived by the hot meat, the bitter coffee, and the brightly colored blankets laid close together warmed by the heated, buried rocks. Even in his anguish at another night in the cold, he knew that he would still sleep well beside the old man.

Cub bedded down next to the tall man as he had done during the two months since he had stumbled upon the lonesome camp of this man of the mountains. With the fire warming his face so close to the earth, the boy's mind raced through their climb into the high country, the meeting in the forest with the stone-faced Painted Elk, the deer hunt, the numbing cold of the great plain, and the tumbling pictures of small-boy dreams.

While the fire crackled at his ear and the old man's steady snoring lulled him, he felt a reluctant gratitude for the old man's having saved the best until the very last. He peered into the darkness toward the cabin where the fire cast shadows on the great notched logs and the glass windows which glowed with reflections red and yellow.

"My Mountain," the boy whispered from the fuzzy edge of sleep under the brilliant stars. Highpockets did not stir.

Cub fought sleep so he could think hard on all that he had seen and all that he had learned along the old man's trail.

Chapter Ten

A DISTANT CLANKING of tinware and the clatter of wood striking wood roused the boy from his deepest sleep in weeks. He turned his cold face toward the warm sun which played on the treetops. He suddenly remembered the little house in the woods and he bolted to his feet. His colorful blankets fell to the frozen ground.

Working at his boots, Cub did not take his eyes from the cabin bathed in the daylight of a new morning. He heard Highpockets banging about inside the cabin. The noise sounded far away since the thin air carried sound only faintly.

"Come, boy!" Highpockets called from inside.

Cub stopped one boy-size step from the porch. He hesitated to invade the old man's world. Highpockets understood.

"Come, Cub. This is our mountain now."

Stepping up, the boy entered the high doorway. He opened his mouth but words would not come. He could only blink.

Highpockets led the boy to a straight-backed chair. The old man lifted Cub's fur cap from his black hair and he pulled tattered mittens from small hands.

Cub looked around at the cabin which now seemed so much larger from the inside than from the outside. The floor was polished wood. Its brown richness shown like glass in the daylight coming through the fine windows.

The doorway was set in the long wall which was broken by glass windows on either side of the door. The boy's wide eyes absorbed hundreds of thick, gold-colored books which lined the long wall from end to end and from floor to ceiling. Except for the door and the window on each side of the doorway, this wall was an unbroken library of immaculate volumes bearing titles set in gold letters upon black spines. The boy could only blink at the books and at the silent old man who nodded his white head at the youth.

The wall opposite the boy met the book-lined, front wall. At the center of this side wall was a massive, stone hearth and chimney. Above a fine fire, the heavy Hawken hung on the stone mantle. The iron was suspended upon wooden pegs which held the rifle hammerside-down. On each side of the chimney, crannies cut into the log wall were lined with wooden shelves holding tinware and cooking pots.

The long wall opposite the front wall had two windows. Close to the wall was one narrow bed. Above the boy, the high ceiling rose to a lofty gable at the center of the large and airy cabin. White mortar glistened between each of the perfectly hewn logs of the cabin.

When the boy turned to face the old man, Highpockets' face cracked into deep furrows highlighted by the firelight and by the morning sunshine streaming through the windows.

"This is what I am," Highpockets said softly as he raised his arm to encompass the bright and cheerful cabin.

Cub was now warm inside his parka and he lifted the heavy furs over his head with Highpockets' help. The old man hung the boy's coat upon one of the wooden pegs in the log walls.

After first closing the heavy door of the cabin against the morning cold, the tall man climbed out of his own parka. In all the time he had known the old man, Cub had never seen him without his furs in daylight. Highpockets hung his wet furs next to the boy's.

After his parka, Highpockets removed a buckskin shirt. He was not wearing long woolies. The boy looked at the big man's skin. He seemed thinner without his furs than the boy would have guessed. Cub's dark eyes stopped at a long, red scar which ran from Highpockets' left side across his gray-haired chest and on up to his right shoulder. The old man felt the boy's eyes upon the ragged wound.

"Vera Cruz, Cub. The Mexican War, March 27th, '47. That's were I met General Pierce that you say is now president. It didn't hurt much."

The old man's eyes glistened and he turned his face away from the boy.

Highpockets pulled a tanned, leather tunic over his bare shoulders. The low sun was brilliant outside the east windows.

Cub walked toward the wall of books. The bindings on the hundreds of volumes glowed where sunlight caught yellow titles set into small, black squares. The boy knew his letters. He had arrived utterly alone in New York City two years ago. Coming to America—the Promised Land to his father—he found work in a sweat shop manufacturing soap. He learned his English there while saving pennies from his nickel-a-day wages for passage west. Wagon fare took 18 months of 15-hour days, six and half days per week. The son of a bookman, the boy touched the books with reverence. He looked toward Highpockets for permission to lift a volume from its place.

"No, Cub. In my books is my treasure, too. Just like yours."

The boy knew from Highpockets' soft and grave tone that his words were for remembering.

"In time, laddy. Come help with the table."

Cub walked to the square table sitting before the hearth. The small table was covered with a delicate, white cloth of lace. He looked up into the worn face for a clue to the many sights around him which were out of character with the old man's hardness. Highpockets laid his large hand lightly upon the tablecloth.

"This was not always mine. It was brought here many years ago." Highpockets stroked the tablecloth. "Now go fetch us some more firewood."

The boy did as he was told and left the cozy cabin for the tall wood pile behind the house. Outside, he stood facing the cabin. Through the glass where imperfections of tempering caused the sunlight to shimmer, Cub watched Highpockets move about the bright cabin. He studied the old man who stashed the contents of his great sack into wall crannies and cupboards. With slow and deliberate care, Highpockets set the boy's bundle of ancient books within a small nook near the single bed. Standing in the cold, the boy knew that he could trust his life and soul to a man who cared so for the books of another.

Cub squinted against the glaring reflection of the morning sun. He watched as the old man held one of the boy's books in his hard hands. Outside, the boy smiled with a puff of steam when Highpockets thumbed through the book in the wrong direction, not knowing that the boy's books read from back to front and that the foreign script read from right to left. Some things even Highpockets did not know. This pleased him.

With an armload of timber, Cub went inside.

"Thanks, Cub."

"You are welcome, Highpockets."

Pausing for a quick meal at the wooden table, the two worked away the day bringing order to the cabin. The hours passed rapidly inside the radiant cabin. Slowly winding down from his feverish pace, Highpockets tended the fire and revived it in the hearth of rough-hewn stone. The wonderful smell of venison brisket in an iron skillet made the boy tired. So he sat down on the narrow bed and sighed when it swallowed him whole.

"Not yet, Cub."

The boy dragged himself to the table where the old man had set his tinware. Cub slumped in his hard chair where he awaited the tall man.

Highpockets sat quietly while the boy said his strange grace. Over dinner, Cub watched the long wall of books behind Highpockets.

As the clearing outside became darker, the old man rose and made a bed for himself on the floor where he laid out a pile of straw mats covered with several of the colored blankets pulled from a steamer trunk. He pointed to the real bed by the wall for the boy.

Highpockets fed the fire as Cub stripped to his long woolies beneath a strange and dirty vest with fringed tassels dangling from its corners. The boy sank audibly into the soft bedding. He felt as if he might disappear into the bed as he pulled the blanket to his chin.

Cub laid there and looked silently at the many magnificent books illuminated in yellow firelight.

Highpockets sat in his chair close to the fire where he enjoyed a pipe. By the time he tapped the pipe against his palm before sliding under his blankets on the floor, his soft "Good night, Cub" was greeted only by the sound of the crackling fire.

Chapter Eleven

CUB LAY AWAKE in the dawn twilight and his sleeping mind returned to distant places and to other times. The wet wood put into the hearth by the old man before daybreak smelled like home and the boy closed his eyes. He drifted across the world to his father's fireplace and to the peculiar light cast by his mother's face. Often while alone and terrified before meeting Highpockets, the boy assuaged his fear by conjuring in his mind the memory of his mother's hands. Everything his mother touched turned into a soft place in the world.

While the boy dozed, Highpockets shuffled about the cabin and had pulled a straight-backed chair toward the fireplace. With a long pipe in his mouth, he sat looking at the wall. The pipe's bowl rested in his right hand and sweet smoke rose above his white hair. The boy had not seen the old man at ease. Highpockets savored every puff. For a long time, Cub watched Highpockets enjoy his smoke. Once, Highpockets reached over and gently touched the lace table-cloth as he watched the firelight flicker on the wall of books.

In a while, Highpockets rose and placed the pipe on the mantle under the suspended rifle. Turning from the stone chimney, he saw the boy's eyes which he greeted with a cheery "Good morning, Cub."

Climbing from his warm bed, Cub looked out the window toward the clearing white with snow and yesterday's boot prints. He covered his woolies with a tattered blouse from which four fringed tassels dangled at his sides.

After breakfast of venison and bitter coffee, Highpockets pulled on his heavy parka and boots. Reluctantly, the boy did likewise.

The old man shouldered a large, flathead axe. He led Cub into the biting cold made all the colder by the thin air.

"Today we chop," Highpockets ordered.

They walked through knee-deep snow to the chopping stump. Cub shivered as the icy air entered the bottom of his parka. All morning, the old man hacked at the log pile. Cub set an iron wedge into each first strike made by Highpockets. The big man beat fir trees into kindling.

After two months together, the boy's command of English amazed the old man. He could understand most of the boy's, thickly accented questions. Cub hung on each of the big man's answers. By noon at the chopping block, the boy had learned that Highpockets had forged My Mountain from the forest many years ago. He had fashioned the cabin from his forest during one vicious winter when early snows prevented the trapper's retreat to the lowlands before the Mexican War.

"Now we eat," was all the old man said when Cub finally asked about the lone rider in the forest, Painted Elk.

After jerky and mid-day coffee, Highpockets returned the flathead axe to its corner by the hearth. He reached for the Hawken above the fireplace. He primed the iron with fresh powder taken from a deep, wooden barrel and he rammed a roundball down the browned barrel.

"Stay close and be still. And we shall make meat for the larder," Highpockets drawled as he led Cub into the snow.

Marching through the snow at the old man's heels toward the trees, the boy had to lift his legs high to plow through the drifted snow.

For two hours, they walked through the snowy forest. They came to the foot of a densely wooded hill. Highpockets pointed to the base of the rise and he gestured to the boy to follow the snowy pass which skirted the hillside. When the hunter started up the hill, Cub hesitated to strike out alone into the trees.

"It is alright, Cub. Meet you on the other side."

Cub made his way around the hill. Every few paces, he looked back to make certain that he could still see the old man climbing in the distance. When the trapper disappeared into the tall trees, Cub shivered with cold and from his fear of being lost forever atop My Mountain.

Cub picked his way through a stand of brown trees heavy with wet snow under gray sky. The wide hill to his left and a steep rise to his right made a narrow pass which the boy followed fearfully. He scanned the ridgeline for Highpockets coming from the other side.

Stumbling over a fallen timber, the boy fell face-down into wet snow. When he spied fresh deer tracks beside his face, he smiled that the trapper had correctly read the woods.

For another hour, Cub walked alone in the gloom. He strained his freezing ears for the Hawken's thunder. When the crack of the rifle did not come, he broke into a gallop around the snow-covered hill. Passing the last deadfall, he nearly collided with Highpockets who stood motionless like another, brown tree. The old man stood there panting out billows of white steam. The boy's breath came in clouds when he asked about the tracks he had followed.

"Just a late-season fawn, Cub. Too small."

The pair made their way back, following Cub's foot prints. When they reached the fresh upheaval of snow shaped like the boy lying face-down, Highpockets smiled and pressed on without a word. He stopped once to kick the snow from a patch of wild onions. The hunter pulled up a fistful of frozen greens.

The gray sky was growing dark as they reached the cabin. The boy was spent. Still clad in his wet parka, Cub fell on the cold bed. Highpockets walked to the fireplace where he hung the heavy rifle. He hung his furs on a wall peg and kindled the fire.

Cub lay exhausted on his back, panting toward the ceiling. He watched his breath rise upward on the cold air until the new fire thawed the cabin.

Wearing a white linen blouse, Highpockets went to the boy and helped him out of his furs.

"Easy, Cub. You're still not used to the thin air up here. Best for you to rest."

Highpockets busied himself at the fire. He place four venison chops and the limp onion greens into a skillet. Outside the windows, the clearing was black. As the boy lay on his side, he watched Highpockets take his pipe from the mantle together with a small leather pouch of tobacco. The old man filled the pipe and lit it with a flaming twig from the fireplace.

Highpockets got comfortable in his large, wooden chair. This was the old man's chair. In the old country, a son never sits in his father's chair. Cub knew that he would never sit in this chair either.

After a time of silent smoking, Highpockets rose and pulled another chair beside his own, close to the fire.

"Here, Cub. Come by the fire."

The sleepy boy shuffled toward the hearth. Sitting in the fire's warmth and the fragrant aroma of the old man's pipe, the boy enjoyed the cabin's peace.

Without talk, they ate the meat. Highpockets refilled his pipe and lit it.

"I shall strike up a bargain with you, Cub. We shall trade stories until we have each heard all there is to hear. Until you go down the mountain come spring. You go first."

For many minutes, Highpockets waited for the boy to sort his thoughts in English. When his words came, Highpockets heard a mixture of thick foreign accents and drawling, mountain English.

The boy spoke slowly about his home in a distant land. He spoke of a widening in a dirt road called Vilna which was home. He told the old man about his father, Yosef the Tailor, a man of faith and of books.

Highpockets had never known a Hebrew before the boy. Except for his tassels at his sides, Cub looked like any other boy who took comfort from speaking of home. He explained with a smile that when his people break both legs, they thank God that they did not break a neck. The old man nodded and smoked as Cub used all of his English for an hour.

Cub stammered. His brow was furrowed as he concentrated on his English. In the old country, Czar Nicholas I of Russia in 1827 passed a conscription law which forced 12-year-old Hebrews into the Russian army for a 25-year enlistment. Mothers often crippled their own sons to avoid the draft. Local officials hired thugs called *khappers* to kidnap Hebrew boys for the army quota in each village. Life in Vilna, Lithuania, became even harder in 1844 when the czar ordered a candle tax on his mother's Sabbath candles.

Then in 1853, the czar made it a crime for Hebrews to wear traditional Jewish clothing. That same year, Cub had turned twelve and the *khappers* came for him. Within days of his birthday, his mother and father had kissed him goodbye, handed him a bundle of books and two candle sticks, and sent him across the continent to a sailing ship bound for America. His parents used their savings from a lifetime of labor to put an ocean between their son and the Russian army. The voyage ended at a New York City sweat shop two years before Highpockets' cabin.

When Cub ran out of English, he sat quietly. He was both warmed and terrified by his memories.

With a long drag on his pipe, Highpockets spoke toward the blazing hearth.

"I was not always called Highpockets. The Blackfoot nation gave me that name long ago when I traded with them and made medicine with them. Who I was in the white man's world makes no difference now.

"I came west before the Mexican War of '47. For a time, I trapped the lowlands. The mountain men along the way taught me the high places. They taught me well: I have not starved. And I still have my hair—after all these years.

"As I came to know the back country, I went higher and higher until I had gone too high to get down when winter came. So I stayed right here. . . . And here I be."

The boy slumped.

"Best turn in, Cub."

Cub waited beneath his blankets in the narrow bed for the old man to tap out his pipe, stoke the fire, and bed down on the floor. But as Highpockets peaceably puffed his pipe, the boy could think only about the wonderfully soft bed.

Chapter Twelve

CUB'S STRENGTH INCREASED daily. He and the old man chopped many piles of wood and they made meat in the dense forest surrounding the cabin. Some days when the sky was clear and purple, Cub could see the jagged peaks far to the west of My Mountain. No longer did he fear leaving Highpockets' side when the old man went high while the boy stalked low to drive the deer toward the trapper who waited atop the snowy hills. If the hunt was fruitless one day, they would return with a gutted buck the next. When the old man walked with a mule deer slung heavily across his back, the boy marched at his heels, proud to carry the heavy Hawken resting in the crook of his furclad arm.

At Highpockets' side, Cub learned to distinguish the pigeon-toed front hoof tracks of the buck deer from the narrower, straight-toed hoofprint of the doe. He learned to set snares for scarce jackrabbits and to dress downed game large and small.

When waiting for the old man to emerge from between the trees, the boy would kneel in the snow to practice striking flint to steel. Along the trek home, Highpockets would stop in white clearings to allow the boy to shoulder the heavy musket and to blast away at a distant stump. At first, the iron's explosion of stinking sulfur smoke frightened the boy. But after his first few weeks atop My Mountain, he came to know the weapon's ways and its blackened, brass fittings. He learned to aim low whenever firing uphill or downhill, and to squeeze the trigger during the precise moment between his heartbeats.

Cub stayed close to Highpockets where he soaked up every crumb of mountain lore which the old man dropped along their way. When they would break out into sunlit clearings in the forest, Cub would make Highpockets' slow circle-in-place to absorb all of the wilderness sign.

During their quiet moments in the forest, Highpockets would often look down at the boy and, with much gravity in his voice, would remind him: "Remember the high places."

As the winter months dragged on, the old man sent Cub high carrying the rifle while Highpockets skirted the base of the steep hills. The first time the boy set the black, iron sights of the Hawken upon a small mulie, he held his breath and tightened his finger on the trigger. But he could not fire. He returned empty-handed to the old man.

"Did you see him, Cub?" Highpockets called as the boy approached from the trees.

"I did," the boy said with guilt in his voice. He waited for the old man's reproach.

"Everything in its time," Highpockets said with a cloud of steam.

Next day, Cub stood alone atop a wooded slope where he squinted over the iron's sights through a cloud of sulfur. The wind carried the smoke over a downed buck felled by the boy's bullet.

The trapper performed the ritual of dressing out the carcass which left a steaming heap of bowels in the red snow.

That night, after dinner of venison and coffee, it was the old man's turn to spin the first story. Cub waited in his chair by the fireplace until Highpockets had filled his pipe.

"I did not always trap, Cub. I had schooling back east where I learned my letters. Before Mexico, I read the law in St. Joe. I wore fine boots and I smelled like a woman.

"I struck a disappointment in the law. I quickly learned that lawyering is helping half of the people to cheat the other half, and helping all of them to cheat the government. So I came to the mountains. I brought my books with me. Then when the war came, I moved on. Because of my schooling I suppose, they made me an officer—a captain.

"After Mexico back in '48, I came back.

"I brought the books all that way because the books were always a comfort to me. I dragged them up the mountain over five summers." He pointed with his pipe toward the front wall. "My treasure is in my books, too. Just like you, Cub."

Cub boy had not yet dared to open one of the old man's fine books.

Highpockets looked at Cub.

"Remember, Cub: If you come back to My Mountain one day, my treasure is in my books." Highpockets' expression darkened and became for an instant the grim resolve of the climb up My Mountain.

Talk of the war in a place called Mexico stirred a new memory in the boy. He stared into the fire which sparkled in his black eyes when he told Highpockets about the wagon train westward four months earlier.

Cub and five young men went into the wilderness to search for a cow which had straggled from the train. Along Deer Creek, 50 miles west of Fort Laramie, an early blizzard struck like a wall of white. The others abandoned Cub when he could not keep up. By the time he found his way back to the Overland Trail, the twenty wagons were burning, the men and boys were butchered, and their mothers and sisters were naked and dead. Cub shivered beside the warm fireplace.

"Sioux?" Highpockets nodded gravely. Cub shrugged. He knew the word.

On August 18th, 1854, the Brule-Sioux put on their war bonnets after an accidental shooting between soldiers and red men at Fort Laramie. Chief Spotted Tail turned himself over to the army as a hostage to prevent reprisals against his people. But bloody raids by soldiers and Sioux continued along the Overland.

"Not Sioux," Cub frowned. "White men in buffalo coats. I saw them. I hid near the river. They burned the wagons." He paused. "And they did the thing to the women before they killed them."

Highpockets raised a white eyebrow when he looked at Cub.

"They told me all about that in New York, at the soap factory."

The old man nodded.

That night, while waiting for sleep to come, the boy thought about Highpockets' story. He did not have to wonder about what treasure could be in the old man's books. Being a book-man, Cub could understand. For the first time since climbing My Mountain, he suffered red and frightful dreams full of men who looked like Highpockets. He remembered the young woman who had been his friend and who had shared her bread with him. He dreamed of her lying face down with a wild man on top who then gutted her like Highpockets would a deer.

Although the days were slowly growing longer, the nights were still freezing.

One cold day, Highpockets and the boy set out into the forest. Highpockets took his great sack filled with blankets and two canteens of water. In his belt, the boy carried the long knife given to him by the trapper. For a full day they walked deeper into the trees than they had gone before. Along the way, Highpockets pointed out fallen timbers and great boulders in the snow. "Mind that," was all the old man would say, pointing to this landmark or that.

An hour before dark, they came to a small clearing beneath forested hills. Highpockets propped the Hawken against a tree before he sat down wearily upon a fallen timber.

"Make camp, Cub," Highpockets ordered.

As the old man watched closely, the boy cleared a small trench in the fresh snow where he piled small logs and dry kindling. He boy searched for rounded stones beneath the snow. After nursing a fire kindled with sparks from flint struck with the flat of his knife, he laid the stones around the base of the fire.

Highpockets nodded when Cub dug shallow furrows in the frozen earth to receive the stones warmed by the fine fire.

After their meal of venison fetched from Highpockets' sack, they settled into their colored blankets laid on the hard ground. Cub waited for the heat of the buried rocks to soothe his cold body.

The boy felt Highpockets sit up beside him.

"Cub: Remember the high places and all that you have learned."

The fire crackled as sleep came quickly.

Opening his eyes to the gray dawn, Cub looked up at dark clouds and swirling snow. He shivered under his blanket.

When Cub rolled over toward the old man, he felt a blind terror unfamiliar for many months.

Highpockets and his bedroll were gone.

Jumping to his feet, the sleepy boy felt a moment's relief that the fire still crackled as if freshly stoked with kindling. Five paces from the fire, the black Hawken rifle stood propped against a tree. Quickly, the boy heaved the heavy iron into his arms.

Thick snow fell and absorbed every sound among the trees. With a shiver not caused by the biting cold alone, the boy realized that he could not see his boot prints leading homeward. He had no idea which direction led to the cabin. He wanted to scream for Highpockets. But he knew that the old man was not within earshot.

Cub hated the old man. But after standing in the new snow and the absolute stillness, he was overcome with determination. He knew that the time had come to remember the high places with all of its lessons.

Returning to his blanket, he dusted new snow from the red cloth. He laid out his knife, a sharpening whetstone, a flint stone, strips of black jerky, and extra mittens. Laying the musket on the blanket, he saw the powder horn dangling from a sapling together with the leather possibles bag. He reached for them.

He opened the bag and dumped its contents on the blanket: roundballs half an inch across for the Hawken, a dozen small pieces of cloth to make patches to hold the lead balls tightly in the muzzle, and a pile of percussion caps to ignite the powder. As the snow fell on his treasures, the boy stuffed them back into the bag. He slung the long straps of the powder horn and the possibles bag over his furclad shoulders.

After breaking camp, he wore his bedroll across his back and the heavy rifle in the crook of his arm. Turning slowly in place, he studied every stump and every rock. Completing his circle, he knew which way to press into the forest. He doused the fire with snow before marching into the woods.

By noon, he stumbled into a clearing. He rested the Hawken on his right boot to keep the stock out of the snow. He held the barrel in his right mitten. He blinked the snow from his eyes and studied the frozen stream bed winding through the trees. Squinting along its path, he hoped to see three large rocks off to one side. Seeing the boulders, he ran toward them over wet snow. He sat on a fallen log where he enjoyed a rest and a strip of hard jerked venison. Revived, he followed the narrow gully into thick tree stands.

With much panting, he climbed a steep slope. Even in the bitter cold, he could feel sweat beading on his face. From the crest of the rise, he examined the forest in all directions. He looked for any clue to the trail home, but he found none.

Grieving with disappointment, he heard the moist floor of the forest behind him. He turned to see a small doe romp into the cover of the trees. Hoping that the little mulie knew the best route downward, he followed her tracks for two hours.

As the sky darkened toward the east, the deer sign ended in a small clearing. Fifty paces ahead, the doe pawed the fresh snow. The snapping of a twig under the boy's boot sent the deer flying into the forest. Moving to where the deer had paused, Cub found a grove of nut-bearing hardwoods. He recognized the stand of trees from yesterday.

With nightfall, Cub could go no further. Having at last found a familiar landmark, he did not fear making camp as his knife and flint fed a tiny puff of smoke where he knelt in the snow.

Come morning, he awoke inside his blankets to cold daylight and clear sky. After breaking camp, he made his way to the top of the nearest rise from which to survey the countryside. He recognized nothing, so all he could do was keep the sun at his back and head westward. By noon, the high sun in the thin air warmed his face although his feet and hands were numb with cold. Far blue peaks were clear against purple sky. At first, each peak looked like all the rest. But squinting into the distance, he recognized the ridge line visible from the cabin's windows. Determined to keep the ridge to his left, he skidded down the snowy slope and followed a wide pass between high hills.

Toward late afternoon of his second day alone, the boy stopped to rest. His heart pounded in his dry throat burned raw from the cold mountain air. He imagined that he knew the tall firs all around him.

As he caught his breath, he heard a far-away wrapping of wood against wood. He shouldered the heavy Hawken and headed toward the sounds.

The sun was low by the time the boy reached a place in the timbers where the sound grew louder with each step. By now, every tree looked familiar. He rested the shooting iron across his arm. He slowed his pace through the forest.

He let his ears lead the way toward the sound of a flat-head axe falling upon a tree-stump, chopping block.

The low orange sun illuminated the top of Highpockets' chimney against the treeline as Cub reached the last steps before the cabin's clearing.

He stopped to catch his breath. The iron axe was stuck deeply into the stump. The old man had his back to the boy where Highpockets was stacking wood on the pile. The boy decided to celebrate his homecoming quietly as would befit a mountain man. So he entered the clearing without a word.

Highpockets turned toward the boy before returning to his wood pile. Cub walked wearily behind Highpockets toward the front porch. Passing the windows, he saw the blazing hearth within. He said nothing.

Dropping his bedroll to the porch, he propped the Hawken against the wall. Behind him, the old man still tended his wood pile.

Cub could wait no longer.

"I am home, Highpockets," he said proudly.

The old man did not raise his smiling face from his work.

"Of course you are, Cub."

Chapter Thirteen

THE BOY WAS too exhausted to sleep. Two days alone in the frozen forest left him with a vague feeling of being somehow changed.

Sitting across from Highpockets by the evening fire, Cub was warmed by roasted venison and hot coffee. With tired, black eyes, he studied every nook and cranny of the cozy cabin.

Highpockets said nothing as he watched the boy take the cabin's measure with new eyes. The old man understood, but he would wait for the boy to know in his own time.

The cabin's windows were black. The wavy glass reflected the fiery hearth and the blue smoke from Highpockets' pipe. When Highpockets removed the pipe from his bearded face, the boy looked over at him to await his words.

"You have come far, Cub. I shall tell you another story tonight. You may save yours for tomorrow."

When Highpockets rose to pile fresh logs upon the fire, the boy pulled a heavy blanket tighter around his shoulders and he squirmed to find a comfortable place in his deep, wooden chair. The big man resumed his place close to the little table with its fine lace cloth. The trapper thumbed the delicate cloth with his hard hand while he held his pipe with the other. He looked into the fire and his words came slowly. The boy closed his eyes the better to see Highpockets' words.

"Long ago, and far away, there lived a very young man. He was older than you, Cub, but much younger than I am now.

"He was not a bad man, mind you, only his dreams were greater than he could carry about. He worked hard to measure up to them.

"He lived out east where everyone lived in neat little boxes. Well, this young fellow could not live in a little box so he went west. After ten—maybe fifteen—years, he needed a change again. When he heard about the war with Mexico, he went south to fight for Texas. He thought it would be a grand fight. Only he did not think that folks would be doing much dying for it.

"But they did a pile of dying. The war was without glory and it stunk of powder and of men blown apart. One day, after he had crawled on his empty belly in the sand for hours, he up and ran. He weren't no coward. It was just all the stinking and the men crying and the bloody pieces of his friends laying in the mud. . . .

"So he ran his heart out for two, maybe three days. Crossed the big river. By and by, he came to Saint Louis. He found others like himself there: men full of dreams. And they had the gold fever something fierce. It was a year or two before the big strike in California.

"They headed west with a wagon train of settlers. Along the way, they learned the ways of the wild country. The young man came face to face with the men of the mountains. He sat at the fires of hard men who knew Jim Bridger. One time he even met a tall, thin trapper who said that he was Elijah Stevens himself. Imagine that! The young man could not be sure, but he might have been Stevens.

"After Saint Joe, they followed the Overland along the North Platte River westward. It took months of hard driving to make Fort Kearny and on up to Fort John north of the Colorado Territory. They trapped and traded their furs at the posts at Ash Point and Fort Laramie and at Deer Creek. Out of Deer Creek, they stood at Independence Rock. There, only the young man dared climb the Devil's Gate before they pushed west to South Pass and the Sublette Cutoff. A month later they were in the mountains at Fort Owens and two weeks after that they crossed the Snake River for Fort Hall."

Lost in his story, Highpockets did not see Cub shudder at the mention of Deer Creek—the place where his nightmares began.

"At Fort Hall, the young man and the others left the Overlanders on the Oregon Trail to head up north as far as their horses and pack mules would take them. They crossed the Snake and rode north. After many weeks, they came to the Little Lost River which they followed up to the Bitter Roots and up to Lost Trail Pass in the Montana country.

"All along the way, the little band fought the Blackfeet: fiercesome warriors and a mighty nation. One by one, the young man's partners got picked off. By the time they crossed the narrows of the South Fork Flathead River, with the Flathead nation to the west and the Blackfeet to the east, there were only the young man and two others left. And all of them carried a roundball or broadhead inside somewhere.

"But their gold fever was worse than any Blackfoot arrowhead. So they cussed and crawled their way into the mountains, so high the red men would not follow. They holed up in the high country all winter. When the deer went low for the winter, the three of them ate their horses every one.

"Come spring, they went down the mountains to where the streams ran with white water and the heavy, yellow metal. They panned until they filled up a saddlebag with gold. Had some flakes big as your thumb.

"After a few months of working the rivers, it was time for them to trade their diggings for powder, tobac, and a once-a-year woman. They loaded up and packed out with their gold slung over their backs. They had long ago eaten their animals. For two months they walked.

"Then one fine morning in Flathead country, the young man woke up in sunshine. He was alone beside a wide river.

His saddlebag was gone and his new Leman .58 rifle was gone. Even his boots were gone. And so were his two partners. They left him nothing but the long woolies on his back.

"All that he had learned in the wild was not wasted and the young man tracked the two brigands for six weeks. Day and night, he read their sign in every broken twig and cold firepit. Sometimes a creek would swallow their trail; but he would find it on the other side. Sometimes, he would not find it for a week. But it did not matter. He always found their sign.

"It was just nightfall when he came upon a sandbar twenty paces from the Clark Fork's fast water. He made his way across the sand leaving bloody footprints which stopped at two parched heads sitting on their chins in the sand. He recognized his partners buried to their lips when he knelt down close enough to see the black blood where their hair had been."

Cub looked at Highpockets who paused to suck his pipe. The boy felt a shiver at the icy hardness in the old man's face.

"First one head then the other opened red, cracked eyelids. Four glazed eyes took a long time to focus on the young man, barefoot and in rags. The blistered lips of the buried heads thanked God for deliverance.

"The two bleeding heads opened their mouths to speak but they could only make terrible, croaking sounds. Things crawled out of their faces.

"The young man limped upon his bare and bloody feet to the river bank where he cupped his raw hands and filled them with water. He went back to the buried bodies and he laid his cupped hands to the lips of each. Like dogs, they lapped at the water from the young man's hands. They licked his fingers. He made many trips back to the river until his partners were brought back to life a little.

"'God help us,' one of the heads cried. But the young man just stood there, looking down at them and at his own bloody feet.

"'Where are my boots?' the young man demanded as darkness fell upon them. 'And where is my iron and my clothes?'"

Highpockets sucked his pipe furiously within a thickening blue cloud.

"'And where is my gold?' he asked.

"One of the buried heads cried out loud. The young man walked to the river and he bathed there. Refreshed, he walked back to his buried companions.

"He knelt and dug a trench, inches from each head. He dug so close to each face that the sand trickled into each mouth. He packed the sand down hard before he went down to the river to fill his cupped hands with cold, clear water. He poured the water into the trench inches from the two cracked tongues reaching like dogs to taste the water—just out of reach. He made many trips to the river until the trench held the water up to the edge.

"The young man stood up in the last daylight. Above the whimpering heads, he walked into the nearby forest. He returned with an armload of kindling which he piled in front of the buried heads and made a pile of tinder half a man high. With two sticks rubbed together furiously, the young man made a fire which sputtered and grew in front of the heads. The firelight danced in the pool of water just under the sunburned faces growing out of the sandbar. The water did not sink out of sight in the wet sand so close to the river.

"The young man sat down beside the sandbar. All night long he just sat there. He stoked the fire and he brought more water to his little trench. All night long he watched the blisters rising on the buried faces which lapped at the water they could not reach.

"Come morning, no sound broke the stillness except for the river. The new sun was wonderful were it fell on four lifeless and broiled eyeballs in the sand. Two mouths were open wide and were full of black tongue. He covered the embers with wet sand and he walked back into the forest."

Beside Highpockets who puffed his pipe, Cub nodded off. The tall man rose to tap his pipe against the hearth.

"The young man walked barefoot for another six weeks to a camp of white men. There, he found his saddlebag, still half full of heavy gold." Highpockets spoke into the fire while Cub slept in the hard chair.

"Before morning, the young man took what was his and left behind a man who must have thought a tree had fallen on his head while he slept."

Highpockets faced the dozing boy. Cub was wrapped to his ears in the great blanket of many colors. His breath came slowly and evenly. The old man laid his pipe on the hearth before he gently picked up the boy. Laying him down into his bed, the tall man pulled the heavy blankets up to the boy's face. Cub did not move.

"My treasure is in my books, too," Highpockets said softly before returning to his fire. He sat alone for a long time.

Chapter Fourteen

WINTER LINGERS LONG in the high country, and the weeks dragged on after Cub's sortie alone into the forests of My Mountain. Although the days were longer, the air was still cold and thin.

Coming and going in My Mountain's timber stands, the boy trailed in the old man's boot prints. He enjoyed the trapper's stories about the vanished Arapahos who once hunted these mountains. They had called themselves the Inunaina people. Highpockets entertained Cub with stories about fancy, English, Lord Dunraven who had tried to raise horses in the high country. He spoke of Rocky Mountain Jim Nugent as if he had known him face to face. Through it all, Cub was becoming a mountain man.

So it was for weeks. As Cub's tales of the old country followed the old man's lessons about the wilderness, the respect which each carried for the other became the kind of love which requires no words.

One clear afternoon, they stood in the narrows of a rocky gorge between two ridges. Highpockets knelt in the snow and Cub held the Hawken. With his bare hands, the old man cleared a patch of snow until a small mirror of ice shone in the fierce daylight. Highpockets raised his fist above his furclad head and his arm crashed down on the ice of a stream bed. The ice shattered and clear, icy water splashed into the brittle air. Beneath the ruptured ice layer, white water surged down the gorge. Water slurped up through the jagged hole in the ice.

"Spring begins here, Cub," said Highpockets softly in a cloud of white steam.

They walked in silence the hour back to their cabin. Not until they reached the clearing by their wood pile did the old man speak.

"With the coming of green to the high places, you will return to the lowlands, Cub. Here will I stay until my time to go."

The boy could not speak.

"When the long days come again to My Mountain, I must go down alone to the council of Painted Elk. You do remember the law giver?"

Highpockets had not mentioned Painted Elk before.

During the following week, Cub noticed that Highpockets stayed closer to the cabin. From time to time, the old man would remove his treasures from the log walls and crannies to wipe dust and soot from shelves and corners. And one by one, the old man gathered up the boy's belongings and he tied them carefully into little bundles. Such days were heavy with silence as the sun rose earlier and set later outside the cabin's windows. Frost still covered the windows and snow still lay on the roof.

One morning Cub awoke to the smell of fresh coffee and hot venison. He rolled over and sleepily watched Highpockets as he puttered about the tidy cabin. Blinding daylight splashed upon the shining, wooden floor through the wavy glass.

"Morning, boy," the old man said cheerfully.

The boy grimaced as his bare feet touched the cold floor.

"Three plates, Highpockets?"

When Highpockets did not answer, Cub turned his back to the old man, and his covered head rocked back and forth. Over the monotonous tones of his morning chant, Cub heard the sudden sound of footsteps upon the front porch. Stunned, he stopped his song. He glanced up at Highpockets who still worked his hearth.

Breathless, Cub watched the old man rise and walk toward the door closed tightly against the night chill. Highpockets showed no alarm in his long, easy stride. Reaching the doorway, he lifted the latch and opened the door.

Wrapping his arms around his body to keep out the blast of cold wind rushing through the doorway, Cub blinked with fear at the towering bear of a man who stood in the doorway. The boy recognized the trappings of the men of the high places: fur from head to toe, dangling possibles bag, and heavy, browned rifle.

The huge visitor and Highpockets were immediately locked in a laughing, rocking embrace which filled the cabin with a roar of manful voices. The boy's cold feet felt the floor vibrate with the bearhugs between the two men.

"You're always welcome at this fire," Highpockets said.

"Much obliged," boomed the stranger as he stepped over the threshold and handed his shooting iron to Highpockets who propped the heavy piece in the corner by the hearth.

"Cub, meet Montana Pete: the best there is."

The boy blinked up at the smiling eyes of the broad stranger in fur parka.

"Damned pleased to make your acquaintance, boy," the visitor called as he took off his furs. The big man put out his bare hand toward Cub who laid his small hand into the cold palm hard as stone.

"Smells like breakfast, Highpockets," Montana Pete said in his deep voice. He stamped his boots on the floor to thaw his legs.

Each big man studied the ruddy and furrowed face of the other. They stood near the little table in the center of the cheery cabin.

"You look well, old friend," Montana Pete smiled. His deep-set, dark eyes twinkled under bushy eyebrows.

"And you, Pete," Highpockets nodded. Before the crackling fire, the two men grasped hands in a four-fisted clasp.

"And you, Pete."

Highpockets gestured for Montana Pete to sit at the table's third plate and for Cub to take his usual place opposite Highpockets.

"This here be Cub," Highpockets pointed. "I found him down below wandering around. Been here all winter together."

"You're a mountain man, too, are you?" Montana Pete smiled toward Cub.

"That he is, for sure," Highpockets replied before the boy could answer Montana Pete's easy smile.

"Seems you were expectin' company," Montana Pete said to the old man.

"You are an easy target, Pete. Been watching your sign near on two weeks now as you climbed."

"Didn't want to startle you, 'Pockets. Didn't want you to greet me with Old Martha ablazin'." Montana Pete nodded toward the Hawken rifle hanging above the fireplace.

"Be staying long, Pete?"

"Reckon long enough to swap a yarn or two, and share a few smokes with you. Them chops sure smell fine," sniffed the bearded guest.

Highpockets rose toward the hearth where venison sizzled and the coffee pot boiled. He laid a large slab of meat upon each of the three, tin plates before he filled three cups with steaming coffee.

"Not yet," Highpockets said softly as he laid his hand on Montana Pete's arm which was reaching for the coffee mug. Highpockets nodded to the boy who closed his eyes to recite his grace quickly. When he had finished, Highpockets picked up his coffee.

Between his animal sounds, Montana Pete paused and exchanged words with his old friend. It had been many months since Highpockets had enjoyed the chatter of another grown man cut from the same hard cloth.

Montana Pete ate with his long, hairy fingers and he spoke as he chewed.

"How's the trappin' been this high, 'Pockets?"

"Sparse, Pete. Most everything seems to have gone low this year. Winter came early and has stayed long."

"Yep," Montana Pete nodded over a mouthful of mule deer. "Seen game low alright. Nothin' for the last three weeks. Least you and the boy ain't starved yet."

"No. We'll not be getting fat up here, for sure. But the table never been empty."

Highpockets finished first and he sat watching his friend wolf down breakfast. A shaft of daylight fell upon the table from the morning sun low in the sky. Montana Pete wiped his mouth on his greasy sleeve and he nodded his approval as he ate.

"Fine eatin'," Montana Pete smiled as he finished and rocked back in his hard chair. "My thanks to you and Cub."

The boy smiled at the big man who had so quickly filled the cabin with good cheer.

"Now," Pete boomed, "what can I do to help?"

"Can always help at the wood pile," Highpockets said.

"Good enough! Let's go, Cub. Old 'Pockets can tend to the woman's work."

The boy pushed back from the table and he dragged on his furs and boots. Montana Pete put on his parka, still cold and damp.

The boy walked into the dazzling daylight of morning in the mountains. As he had done for five months, Cub handed thick logs to Montana Pete who stood with the flathead axe in hand beside the chopping stump. As wood chips filled the air, Cub was amazed at the big man's power. Pete's broad back made Highpockets look small.

As his axe fell heavily, Pete spoke to the chopping stump.

"So now you be a mountain man, too?" Pete said with a solid *whack!* of the axe which the boy could feel in his feet.

"Old Highpockets and I go way back together." *Whack!*

"We weren't much more than boys when we met down in the plains." *Whack!*

"Does seem like yesterday." *Whack!*

"We trapped together many summers. Then I went low and Highpockets went high." *Whack!*

"When 'Pockets dragged all them books up the mountain, I helped him for two summers. Never did think he would make it." *Whack! Whack!*

Montana Pete took aim and demolished each log with two strokes at most of the axe. By the time the sun was high in the south at noon, Cub stood next to a pile of freshly split wood as tall as himself. The big man panted hard in the thin, cold air.

"Old 'Pockets tell you about the treasure, Cub?"

Cub looked up at the tall man who rested leaning on the axe handle.

"Damn good hiding place, don't you think?" Pete laughed. When the boy only blinked, the big man sensed that Cub was not privy to all of My Mountain's secrets. So Montana Pete shouldered the axe and led him toward the cabin.

Lunch of coffee and jerked venison already sat on the table. When the three sat at table, Pete waited for the boy to mumble his peculiar grace. Cub was silently impressed with how quickly the tall, loud stranger had accommodated his foreign ways.

Compared with breakfast, they ate quietly. Cub took silent note that the cabin was very tidy. It troubled him that Highpockets brought more order to the cabin with each new day.

"Come, Cub," Montana Pete called after he wiped his face on his sleeve. "Time for a walk."

Pete stood up and fetched his damp parka from its peg in the log wall. All Cub wanted was a nap after his morning in the cold by the wood pile. But he climbed back into his furs.

Montana Pete stood by the closed door. His buffalo rifle rested in the crook of his arm. When Cub shuffled toward the door, Highpockets gestured for him to wait. Then the old man gently lifted his Hawken from its pegs above the hearth. For nearly half his life, Highpockets had called the weapon

"Old Martha" and he handed it to the boy whose arms dropped under the weight of ten pounds of steel, polished wood, and shining brass. In the lowlands, the brass furniture of trigger guard, patch box in the wood stock, and the brass thimbles which hold the ramrod to the barrel, are all charcoaled black over a fire. This keeps the sun from glinting on the metal to give a white man's position away to those who would like his hair on a coupstick. But in the high country, Highpockets brushed Old Martha's brass until it glowed.

Cub took the iron in his mittens. He said nothing when Highpockets handed him the powder flask and the possibles pouch. Montana Pete pushed him through the door and they crossed the snowy clearing quickly.

"Powder up, boy," Pete's deep voice rolled through the calm forest. Surrounded by tall firs, Cub charged Old Martha with black powder. He measured out just enough powder to cover a lead, roundball in his palm, the standard hunting charge for mountain men. The ball wrapped in patching cloth was rammed down the barrel after the powder. Then Cub fumbled inside his possibles bag for a tiny percussion cap to place under the eared-back hammer.

With their irons lethal, they pressed deeper into the tree stand. After an hour of walking in silence, they came upon feathered battle lances sticking in the snow. Cub had seen many when walking in the forest with Highpockets. The footprints near the lance were new and were not yet filled with snow. Pete stopped to regard the lances but he dared not touch them. He knew bad medicine when he saw it. Just as Highpockets had always done, Pete walked wide around the lances and he let them be.

"You take the high country, Cub. I'll take the base of yonder hill. If'n you spook a buck or a spike, aim well and dispatch 'im clean, boy."

Before the boy could respond, Montana Pete disappeared into the trees, leaving him alone in the early spring cold. Shifting the heavy, shooting iron from one arm to the other and back again, Cub climbed a steep slope. Every few steps he had to grab a sapling to keep from sliding backwards. The woods were dead quiet and gloomy as the thick fir trees filtered out much of the late afternoon sunlight. Every twenty paces, he stopped to switch arms under the rifle.

After half an hour of hard climbing, Cub reached the summit. He studied the treeline for any trace of Montana Pete. But he was alone absolutely.

The snow underfoot was wet. Looking upward, he noted that the firs' limbs had very little snow on them. "Spring comes late and comes slow this high," Highpockets had said.

For an hour, he waited at the crest of his ridge. He squatted behind a fallen timber and looked down slope into the cold, damp wind which he knew to keep at his face. At the base of the hill was a cluster of saplings. Any game coming from the trees would have the wind at its back: a fatal blunder.

In the perfect stillness, Cub raised his weapon to the ready and laid the muzzle gently on a small stump. He grimaced when he laid his face against the bitter cold stock of the Hawken.

Crouching in the wet snow, Cub squinted over the rifle and thought about killing his next meal. His father's ancient people believed that Death comes for a body by the Angel of Death who stalks his prey by name. For that reason, at the hour of one's death the rabbi is summoned to the bedside to change the name of the dying. Changing the victim's name might confuse the angel. Now the boy was the angel. He shivered.

A rustle from the brush alerted him. Twigs snapped under the weight of four small hooves. Cub wished that the thin air would explode with the thunder of Montana Pete's rifle.

As the sound came closer, Cub's ungloved fingers tightened on the Hawken. A brown nose sniffed from the trees thirty paces from the boy hunter crouching in the underbrush. Wide antlers followed. A shaft of brilliant sunlight fell on the animal's shoulders when it left the safety of the trees for the clearing at the base of the boy's hillside.

Holding his breath, the boy saw the flash of his iron and his shoulder was stung by the recoil. The doomed deer and the trees behind were lost in a stinking cloud of sulfur and tiny red sparks. The wind blew the stench back into Cub's numb face.

Cub's muscles ached as his face pressed against the stock of his weapon. Down the slope, the mulie lay in the shallow snow. Dark blood oozed from the hole drilled into the buck's brown chest.

Before he reached the red snow, Cub saw Montana Pete come out of the trees.

"You done well and clean, Cub," Pete nodded.

Together they advanced to the carcass. The tall man took the boy's rifle which was blotched with moist rings of condensation caused by the heat of the powder explosion. When Montana Pete handed the boy his knife, the young hunter studied the flat blade.

As Pete held both irons, Cub knew that he had to finish what he had started, after first thanking the sky for filling the larder. Montana Pete sat down on a stump and cradled the rifles on his lap to protect the meat-givers from the snow.

Cub dressed out the slain animal whose innards steamed when warm flesh fell limply out onto the cold snow. He worked quickly as his white breath rose toward the darkening sky. Such is the way of mountain men.

Chapter Fifteen

THE STARS AND the moon lighted their way by the time Montana Pete and Cub ended their first day together. The dirty snow of the cabin's clearing was illuminated by the firelight behind the windows.

Cub stumbled exhausted against the porch step. The tall man carried the gutted deer across his back and the boy carried twenty pounds of rifle in his arms.

When Cub pushed the cabin door open, Highpockets filled the doorway. So intense was the light from inside that the edges of the old man's shape shimmered to the boy's snowblind eyes.

"You did well, Cub," Highpockets said as he looked at the deer carried by Pete. Neither hunter had told Highpockets whose roundball had brought the buck down. But the old man somehow knew.

Highpockets took the shooting irons from the boy. Montana Pete heaved the mulie to the top of the front porch roof where the cold night would keep it fresh until they could quarter it.

Montana Pete entered last to remove his furs wet with snow and deer blood. By the time Pete had stripped to his soft buckskins, Cub already lay face-down in his drawers on the narrow cot.

"Boy done just fine, 'Pockets," Pete said to the old man who was busy setting three plates at the little table.

"Aye, that," Highpockets said into the deep, wooden trunk where he knelt. He rose with three tin cups in his hand.

Cub sighed as he turned his face toward the cabin so he could watch the two men who shuffled in the firelight. The cabin seemed smaller when filled with Montana Pete. The tall stranger smiled at the boy as he took his place at the table. He sat with his back to the doorway and the wall of books. Highpockets sat down and he called to the boy.

"Too tired, Highpockets. Please."

Cub raised his dark eyes to the old man who smiled. When Highpockets nodded, Cub pulled his colorful blanket up to his chin.

Lying close to the wall, the boy did not remember dozing off. But when he opened his eyes, the cabin was dimly lighted by the fire in the hearth and the room was fragrant with pipe smoke. Cub turned his face toward the hearth to see Highpockets and Montana Pete sitting on either side of the table by the fireplace. Both hard and furrowed faces were in clouds of sweet, white smoke where they puffed on their pipes. The two old friends of the high country cut a fine picture in the tranquil and cozy cabin. Their talk was soft.

"I dunno, 'Pockets. Even honor has its limits," Montana Pete said through his pipe smoke.

"What limits, Pete? You know how many men I judged. Did I ever allow others to limit their honor in my courtroom? I ran a hanging court."

"I know, alright. But you were younger then and full of yourself. We were both younger. You read the law; that was all. It was the law what locked men up, not you."

"All I did was hide behind the long black robe. Besides, I sent you up, didn't I?" Highpockets had a tight, little smile on his hard face when he looked at his old friend.

"That you did. But I was tried fair and square. You always made sure of that. Yessir: fair and square."

In his bed beside the log wall, Cub labored silently to sort out the drawling, mountain English falling softly upon his ears.

"So now, 'Pockets, you think you can make up for all of that by going to the council of Painted Elk? It just makes no sense."

"But it does, Pete: I sat in judgment upon others by my own rules. Painted Elk and his council will sit in judgment of me by their rules. Where is the difference? Whose way is better? I don't know anymore. I do not want to know anymore. The boy over there talks to God. I think maybe He answers him, too. I don't hear voices anymore. Maybe Painted Elk does. I hope so."

Cub heard Highpockets' long sigh as both men puffed in silence for many minutes while the boy fought sleep.

"Maybe Painted Elk is the better judge, Pete. Either way, perhaps I can find some peace there."

"I do hope so, my friend. I surely do."

Someone rose and shuffled toward the hearth. As fresh logs brought the blaze to life, Cub felt the heat on his neck where he lay facing the wall. He heard the wooden chairs creak as the two large men got comfortable and enjoyed their smoke.

"Otherwise, 'Pockets, how are you?"

"Well enough. The boy is good company. What about you?"

"Kind of stiff in the knees anymore. But I get by. Only slower." Pete smiled.

"I know the feeling."

"And the treasure, Highpockets?"

The boy opened his eyes as he listened from the warm edge of sleep.

"Right where you and I left it, Pete." Highpockets drew on his pipe and his clear eyes twinkled. "You carrying a squaw these days?"

"You know the likes of me," Pete laughed through his pipe smoke, "my once-a-year woman at the Fort Bridger

Rendezvous just about carries me through the winter. That, and a splash of the squeezins."

"Truly, Pete?"

"Well, now. Guess there was one special gal. It was a while back. There was this little Ruskie girl. She sang in a saloon some'eres near Seattle. A chorus girl, she was. Reckon I do recall her face. A chorus girl. Her name was Eurochka Anna. Sometimes, her face still comes to me. And her voice: Eurochka sang like a bird, like the wind comin' through the trees. When I am alone and cold, I think of her song and I am cold no more."

Pete swallowed hard and he turned his face away.

"I know, Pete. Believe me."

Silence followed. The stillness was broken only by the tapping of warm pipes against the stone hearth. Cub knew that day was done at last so he closed his eyes. With the fresh fire warm on the back of his neck, the weary boy in the narrow bed stopped listening.

A curious dripping sound above Cub's head roused him from deep sleep. In the bright daylight of late morning, he opened his eyes. He could hear Highpockets and Montana Pete talking softly. Sitting up in his snug bed, Cub pressed his nose against the frosted glass. The cold window stung his face. Wiping frost from the wavy glass, he could make out a shallow puddle in the snow outside where dripping water ran down the eaves of the cabin roof.

Spring! the boy thought.

He turned toward the two men who were fully dressed in their soft leathers. Coffee cooled in the tin pot atop the table. Before he could exclaim his pleasure at the newest sign of coming green, his voice caught in his dry throat. He saw Highpockets quietly wrapping more of Cub's belongings into small, neat bundles in the cabin corner beside the hearth. The boy turned his face to the window. He wanted to shout for joy: Spring is coming! But he could not.

"Come get your coffee, Cub," Highpockets called cheerfully from his corner.

"Venison be hot, too, Cub," Montana Pete added loudly.

"Good morning, Highpockets. Pete." Cub spoke with thickly accented words. His Russian always got the best of his morning tongue before it was coffeed.

"Hurry, Cub. We have miles to go before nightfall and Highpockets' table."

Cub was relieved by Pete's assurance that he would see Highpockets again this day. After his morning blessings and breakfast, he climbed into his boots, furry leggings, and bulky fur parka. Inside his furs, Cub walked awkwardly toward the mantle above the fresh fire. He pulled the Hawken from its pegs on the chimney and looked at Highpockets. When the old man nodded, Cub put the strap of the powder flask over one shoulder and Highpockets' possibles pouch over the other shoulder.

Cub followed Montana Pete into the overcast daybreak.

"Till later, Highpockets," the boy called over his shoulder.

"Till later, boy."

All day Cub walked at Montana Pete's side through the dense trees. Long pine needles dripped with the coming of spring to the high places. By nightfall, Cub collapsed on his cot too exhausted to be hungry.

And so it was for three weeks: Every dawn, he followed Montana Pete to some distant and different reach of the surrounding forests.

Whenever Cub had a mulie squarely in the Hawken's sights miles from the cabin, Montana Pete would always manage to snap a twig or cough just in time to send the deer flying into the wilderness. Cub tired of this daily, senseless ritual of going home empty-handed and cold.

But every day Cub followed Pete into the woods. The forest was now alive with new sounds as every tree dripped snowmelt onto the darkening floor of the forest.

As Highpockets was the boy's teacher, Montana Pete was his examiner. What the old man had taught him, Pete was testing in the forest. With each day, his respect for Pete increased. He tested Cub but said very little. He simply followed and watched and listened. Montana Pete's loud "Well done, laddy!" was as welcome as Highpockets' nod of approval.

Pete was pleased by Cub's ability to point out the tall, thin, blue spruces and other trees by name. With the coming of spring, Cub saw life which he had not seen before. Pete pointed out Cub's first Rocky Mountain jay atop an old fir and his first, whiskered, gray marmot. Cub would not have noticed the white ptarmigan grouse had not Pete pointed to the treetops. From time to time, the chirp of a squirrel-like pika broke the quiet woods where the only sound was the dripping of the slow thaw. The floor of the forest was turning a muddy brown where snow had melted. Eddies of ice water ran down slippery gullies.

Montana Pete took him deep into the forest. One evening, Pete ordered him to make camp among the tall spruces. Pete did nothing to help but he took silent note of all Cub did. Not until Cub kindled a fine fire and laid a pile of stones by the flame to warm did Pete smile "Well done, laddy."

After dinner, they sat under a clear sky. Montana Pete puffed his pipe while Cub droned his evening prayers. Pete said nothing.

They crawled into their blankets warmed by heated rocks which Cub had planted underneath. Laying beside Pete in the chill calm, Cub felt the stones warm his weary bones as an uncomfortable dampness oozed up from the thawing earth.

"Tell me, Cub," Montana Pete asked softly, "Where is the cathedral for these prayers of yours?"

In the firelight, the mountain man saw the boy point toward the sparkling sky above their fire. Only Cub's face and mittened hand poked out of his bright blankets.

Montana Pete nodded silently moments before they both slept on it.

With the coming of another damp and cold dawn, Pete rose first to pile dry kindling on the dead fire. When Cub stirred, he was glad to see the tall man helping.

Montana Pete pointed to a feathered, battle lance which stuck in the soft ground ten paces from the boy's face.

"They're gone, boy. Just wanted us to know they was here. That's all. Wash some jerky down with this here coffee and we better be movin' on."

The long march home was chilly and damp. They walked along a trail which was different from the one which led them into the forest. Pete watched Cub as he reckoned his way home by studying the far-off ridge lines and by noting which side of the pines were covered with moss (always the north side).

"Highpockets is as good a man as there is," the tall man said behind the panting boy who led the way. Cub was startled by Montana Pete's voice after hours of silence. Only the big man's silence told Cub that his course was straight and true.

"The world has always been hard for him," Pete continued. "Hard and lonesome. That's why he has carved out his own quiet place. A man must have a quiet place. Even a mountain man."

Pete spoke to Cub's back and the boy said nothing. He had learned from Highpockets that a man says nothing when his thoughts are too big for his mouth.

They plodded homeward for a long day with few words between them. Only the sloshing of their boots broke the silence. A fine, spring mist dripped from low clouds to give the thin, afternoon air an eerie stillness.

Chapter Sixteen

THE CHILL DAMPNESS of night had fallen over Cub and Montana Pete by the time they arrived at their little cabin nestled in the forests of My Mountain. The windows cast long shafts of yellow light onto the dirty, wet snow. Cub's feet were soaked from puddles of slush.

Pete entered the cabin first. When they closed the cabin door behind them, they saw Highpockets sitting in his great oak chair beside the table. Like everything else in the cabin, the old man must have dragged his furniture up My Mountain on his back or else whittled it from the trees.

Highpockets did not rise as Pete hung his damp parka on its peg and propped his shooting iron in the corner near the hearth. Cub stood in the middle of the room where he was stricken by the perfect order all around him.

The cabin was immaculate. Cub looked at the deep lines creasing Highpockets' face inside a blue cloud of pipe smoke. In the old man's eyes Cub saw a terrible sadness.

It was time.

Walking silently across the shining floor, Cub returned the rifled musket, Old Martha, to her place on the chimney wall. Then he shuffled to his bed where he sat down to pull off his boots. He worked at his boots and leggings, but his mind was elsewhere. In the lonesome high places, everything comes in its own time. And everything goes away in its own time.

Now it was Cub's time to go and he could no more change that than he could stop the slow retreat of the snow.

When Cub rose and walked his parka to its peg on the wall, Highpockets leaned toward the fire to fetch dinner of venison steaks.

Over the little table, Highpockets said nothing as he picked at his plate. His head was bowed. Wisps of silver hair fell across his wrinkled brow and he did not raise his eyes to the boy at his side. During the two days of Cub's hike into the forest with Pete, Highpockets had aged.

"It is good to have friends," Montana Pete said softly.

"Good, indeed," Highpockets added, raising his face to meet the boy's black eyes.

When they finished, the old man cleared the table where Pete and Cub waited. Highpockets laid another log into the fire before he walked to the wall of books around the doorway. With a mother's gentle touch, Highpockets lifted a volume from its shelf. The book was elegant with cloth binding and gold letters stamped into a black, leather strip for the title. Highpockets looked at the boy.

"Cub, like you, my treasure is in my books."

The old man handed the volume to Cub. With great care, Cub opened the heavy book.

When he opened it, his breath would not come and his eyes were wide. Between the pages he found a thin sheet of beaten gold. He lifted the shining foil between his fingers. The palm size, gold leaf fell softly over his fingers like shiny silk. Cub glanced up at Montana Pete who grinned knowingly.

Cub laid the gold leaf back between its pages. He turned to the next page where he found another sheet of pure-gold foil. With each page it was the same. He boy looked to Highpockets.

"Aye, Cub."

The boy rose from his chair as if in a dream and walked to the solid wall of books surrounding the cabin's doorway and front window panes. Returning the heavy book to its shelf, he pulled down another volume from a different shelf. More golden leaves glowed in the firelight. In book after book, he found a pound of gold foil.

Stepping back from the hundreds of volumes of weathered books from the old man's other life, Cub searched Highpockets' furrowed face. The old man raised his hand through the warm air in the direction of his library.

"Every book, Cub: my treasure. Just as I said."

Words would not come to the boy. For half a year, he had lived beside enough gold to fill Solomon's temple.

Highpockets stood very close to Cub, close enough for the boy to feel the tall man's breath on his upturned face. The old man laid a hard gently on each of Cub's shoulders.

"Here my treasure will stay, Cub. Until the day when you are grown and you—or your kin—come again to My Mountain. You will be welcome at this fire always." Highpockets sighed deeply. "Kindly take care of my books and my treasure, as I have taken care of yours."

Cub swallowed hard.

"Now, it is late, Cub. You must sleep."

"But, Highpockets," Cub stammered.

"To bed with you. Sleep well in the company of your friends."

Highpockets pushed him toward his bed by the wall where the blanket of many colors had hung all winter. But the blanket was gone now. Highpockets had folded it atop the boy's bundled belongings in the corner. Cub did not look to that corner of the cabin as he climbed wearily out of his cloths. In his long woolies with the dangling fringes at his hips, he softly thanked the God of his father's house for bringing him to another night. In words unknown to Highpockets or to Montana Pete, he also thanked heaven for his friends.

Cub pulled his blanket over his chin and turned his face to the wall to conceal the tears running down his face. He could hear Highpockets and Pete shuffle to the mantle where they filled their pipes before taking their chairs close to the blazing hearth. Sweet smoke soon reached Cub's face and he breathed deeply to suck it in, down to his heart.

"You be the stubbornest of men, 'Pockets," Pete said softly through a breath of blue smoke.

"You are not?" Highpockets chuckled.

"May be. But I have kept my hair damn near sixty years. And I'll not be volunteering to give it up, neither."

"You know that I have fought my fair share, Pete. Usually won, too."

"Then why stop now? You're an old man. I just don't reckon the price of your cussed honor, that's all."

"No price, Pete. I'm just plain tired of judging everyone else. The council of Painted Elk thinks it's time that I be judged. Let them. Simple enough."

"For the love of God, man! They'll eat your liver raw—while you watch!" Montana Pete argued softly through clenched teeth lest he awaken the quiet boy who soaked up every word.

"So be it," Highpockets sighed. "I have eaten my share of theirs."

Cub thought he could hear the old man laugh softly.

"So when will you go down, 'Pockets?"

"Soon as the thaw comes up fully. A month, maybe two."

Cub fought sleep beside the wall. But he was losing in his snug blanket and the warm cabin.

"Take whatever you want, Pete. You could live long and fat on two of my books."

"What would I do with gold? You know the likes of me: The mountains provide all I need. But I am thankin' you."

The two, hard men smoked in silence. Each took the company of an old man's memories which keep him warm in the coldest night.

"Come, Cub." The voice belonged to Highpockets and the painful glare in the boy's sleepy eyes was a brilliant dawn.

When the boy's bare feet stuck to the floor, he felt cheated and angry that sleep had robbed him of his last precious hours atop My Mountain.

Breakfast of venison steaks was already cooling beside three tin cups. Steam rose toward the gabled ceiling.

Cub looked glumly at his plate.

"The blessing, Cub?" Highpockets reminded the boy.

"I do not feel like it, today," Cub mumbled without raising his face.

"Cub, do you want your father's house to end with you?"

Like a knife with ragged edges, the old man's words pierced his breaking heart. So he choked out his little prayer before they ate in silence.

While Cub finished the meat which warmed him to the quick, Montana Pete pulled on his long fur coat and shouldered his sack of wares and his rifle.

Cub looked up toward Highpockets who stood in the corner by the bundles. The boy's throat was as dry as his empty plate.

For a moment, Cub hoped that Montana Pete would be leaving alone. But when Highpockets nodded, Cub stood and climbed into his boots, furry leggings, and heavy fur parka. Outside, the morning wind blew with mountain chill across the melting snow which still lay in the high passes.

Cub stood beside Pete near the wall of books which concealed a king's ransom in gold.

Pete perspired in the warm cabin. Cub slouched under the burden of his own deep sack stuffed with blankets, jerked venison dried in strips on the hearth, and his father's ancient books carefully packed by Highpockets. Somewhere on the boy's back were his mother's silver candlesticks newly shined by the old man.

Highpockets reached for his rifle hanging on the hearth's mantle. Cub noticed that the once shiny, brass fittings were well blackened with soot.

Montana Pete stepped from the boy's side as Highpockets approached carrying his trusted rifle.

The old man's sad eyes met those of Montana Pete.

"You take care of your hair, Pete."

"And you, old friend."

Highpockets laid the heavy shooting iron into Cub's mittened hands. When the old man laid the strap of the possibles pouch over his shoulder, Cub choked back tears. He looked up into Highpockets' eyes, gray and glistening.

"For you, Cub," Highpockets said as he released the rifle into the boy's hands. "Protect Old Martha as she has protected us and made meat for us. Keep your powder dry."

Cub took the Hawken into his hands as one tear rolled down his face.

"Highpockets?" Cub raised his wet face toward the old man. "Have I done well?"

The old man smiled his kindly, weary smile.

"Cub, I wish I had known your father."

The boy felt new strength deep within and his fingers tightened on the rifle.

Cub turned to follow Montana Pete through the open door into the brilliant morning. He heard the old man at his back call softly and hoarsely.

"Remember the high places!"

Neither Pete nor Cub looked back as the cabin beneath the tall firs disappeared when the pair entered the trees beyond the muddy clearing.

Cub could not see Highpockets standing in the open doorway. The old man stood there quietly until his friends were gone from view. When Highpockets entered his empty cabin, he left the door ajar.

The chilly wind from the purple sky whistled through the open door, washing over the old man who sat alone beside the table. His stony face looked out at the footprints and at the tall trees and the distant blue ridges.

Chapter Seventeen

NO OTHER WHITE man had been permitted to know the ancient hot springs where Highpockets bathed in the dazzling sunshine. Clouds of dense white steam boiled into the violet sky. The small pool of salty water was fifty paces around and the old man floated to his naked shoulders in the hot brine.

In his youth, Highpockets had enjoyed the hot springs at Telluride and at Ouray in the Colorado territory. Once, he rode by horse as far into the Montana country as Livingston's hot springs. He had also left his mark at the springs known to the men of the mountains as Hookers' Dirty Socks and as Oh-My-God. But he was so much younger and harder then.

The hot water boiled up in the thin, mountain air around Highpockets. The high salt concentration buoyed Highpockets and he floated flat on his back. The spring had long been the old man's secret place. He had shared it neither with Montana Pete nor with the boy, both gone now for a week.

In the days following the return of silence to My Mountain, Highpockets had carefully quartered and dried the deer which Montana Pete had left behind. That done, he had rubbed piles of coarse salt into the hide to preserve it until he could tan the hide with alum into new buckskins. He had also scrubbed and tidied the cabin until there was nothing left to do.

Highpockets closed his eyes. The hot water suspending him carried him into the shadow halfway toward sleep. His white beard rested upon his gray-haired chest and a chill wind blew through his shoulder-length gray hair. He felt old, especially those parts which showed. Without the boy to charge his heart, the old trapper needed the hot springs to soothe his stiff joints in the chilly springtime of My Mountain. Knowing that the small parties of red men who scouted his every move would not violate his privacy, he dozed under his purple sky.

The sun was low atop the spruces to the west when the old man opened his eyes. With much effort, he hauled his naked and battered body from the hot pool. Standing barefoot in the dirty snow hit him like the shock of birth.

The clearing was dark by the time Highpockets arrived home. He quickly built a fire in the stone hearth after first saving a handful of the fine, white ash from which to render soap from the fat of the deer left behind by Montana Pete.

He supped on venison and hot coffee. He resolved to fetch one more mule deer from the forest before he headed down his mountain. When he had cleared the table and stoked the fire, he carefully removed the white lace cloth from the table. From a nook in a cabin wall, he retrieved a black revolver and laid the handiron on the wooden tabletop. With a rag, he cleaned the 2½ pound, 1850 Navy Colt. He rubbed every inch of the 7½ inch, octagonal barrel and the .36 caliber, six-ball chamber.

He charged the cleaned iron with 30 grains of black powder in each chamber behind six marble-size balls. He pressed percussion caps onto the iron nipple of each chamber. Then he hung the weapon on the hearth peg where his rifle had hung for half a lifetime. Standing beside the mantle, he filled his pipe. Its mouthpiece perfectly fit his teeth.

Highpockets gently laid the table cloth back where it belonged and then, alone by the fire, he sat and smoked. He did not sleep and a heavily overcast dawn found him sitting in his hard chair.

Although the wind was still chilly and patches of snow lay on the forest floor, spring was in the air. Every day, the old man walked his forest in search of new green. Brown earth emerged from the snow and buds sprouted on branches long asleep.

Each day, Highpockets trekked a different stand of My Mountain's trees. One clear noon, he leaned to rest against a thin aspen. He stood atop a steep ridge from which he could see the lowlands in all directions. He turned in a complete circle and squinted from horizon to horizon. Close by, he spied a fresh battle lance at the foot of the slope where he stood. His heart quickened. The lance had not been there with its waving eagle feathers the instant before.

"I am here!" Highpockets bellowed into the trees where a single hawk dove out of sight at the old man's cry.

"I am here!" the mountains echoed back.

"Do you hear me? I am alive!" he shouted at his sky and the wind answered, "I am alive."

Highpockets walked home in his own muddy boot prints which wound through miles of slender firs and aspens. His dinner of venison and coffee by the flickering hearth ended the choice cuts of his last deer. On the morrow, he would take his old revolver afield and make meat.

The bright sun was orange and low in the clear sky as Highpockets stepped off the front porch. Less than an hour into the trees, he came upon fresh deer tracks winding between the spruces. He followed the sign. True to its nature, the buck kept to the snowy lowlands of least effort while he kept his nose into the cool wind. With the breeze in the old man's face, the hunter knew that he could advance until the wind shifted.

When the deer sign crossed a narrow stream surging down a rocky gorge, the old man left the trail to make a long circle up the slope to get above the hoof prints. He knew that the mulie would not be likely to look upward as he ambled toward his bed.

Highpockets reached the top of the forested ridgeline in early afternoon. He crouched on stiff legs where the rise gave him a clear view of the narrows below. Drawing the old hand-iron from his fur coat, he eared back the revolver's hammer behind one of six, ready roundballs. Kneeling in the last of winter's snow, the hunter examined the weapon's cylinder where it faced the barrel. Satisfied that a thick layer of bear fat still covered the six, primed chambers to prevent an explosive "chain fire" when the weapon was fired, the old man waited.

Down the slope, a large buck pawed at the snow to root out any green beneath. As Highpockets held his breath, the old mule deer snorted loudly and perked up his brown ears. The trapper did not raise his handiron as he squinted into the bright sun to watch the buck's tail which lay flat against his hind quarters. If the animal raised his tail in fear, Highpockets knew that he would have to fire instantly before the deer took flight.

The buck snorted again and lowered his face to graze. Above the deer, Highpockets raised his weapon in both hands. He steadied the piece in his bare fists. His woolen mittens lay in the muddy snow.

For many minutes, the old man held his fire twenty paces above the deer. Looking down the blued barrel of the revolver, Highpockets watched the old animal balancing his heavy rack on his fine, brown head. The animal kept his rump toward the hunter and his nose into the wind. The hunter watched.

The weary trapper felt kinship with his prey. The animal's massive antlers told Highpockets that this buck was not new to the high country. Like Highpockets, the buck had known many barren winters of bitter cold and meager foraging. Like the old man atop the hill, the animal knew the forest and all of its signs. He had not survived the winters and the wolves and the mountain men by being careless. Until this instant.

Highpockets had not lowered his heavy, shooting iron. It grieved him to take the old animal's life. Like the hunter, the buck was old and his face was graying. Like Highpockets, he longed for the coming of the green and of the lengthening days. For the blink of an eye, age communed with age. Highpockets wished for younger prey to walk into his sights. Holding his breath, the old man squeezed the trigger. With the stinking cloud of sulfur filling his mouth, he fired again down the hillside.

Two lead balls screamed past the cloud of bitter smoke and thudded into the front shoulder of the buck. The animal had jerked upright as the crack of the two explosions rolled down the hill a quarter second before the hot lead plowed into him.

The old animal did not fall. He staggered to his injured side. He knelt upon his front knees very slowly. As if oppressed by a great weight, the buck rested his forehead in the dirty snow as the blood came to the two holes in his left shoulder. With a loud snort, the buck heaved himself upright and turned his face toward Highpockets who was skidding down the snowy hillside. He blinked at the old man who slid out of the thinning cloud of acrid smoke which hung on the slope.

Ten yards from the swaying deer, the old man could see the blood oozing from the hurting animal's nostrils which told the hunter that the wound was mortal.

Highpockets raised his handiron ten paces from the animal. The buck reared up and turned full around in mid-air. He bolted five leaps away. On his last vault toward the cover of the trees, the deer came down stumbling. His foreleg struck the soft earth and Highpockets could hear the shoulder bones snap when the animal rolled over upon the two, bleeding holes into a brown heap, dead.

Highpockets returned the warm iron to his belt. He took no pleasure from filling his larder with the dead creature with which he had shared the high places. Kneeling in the snow, Highpockets dressed out the buck quickly lest the meat be allowed to spoil in an intolerable act of disrespect.

Carrying the heavy carcass back toward the cabin, the old man fell into the mud many times. He cursed aloud his aching body for its lost youth.

Not until midnight did Highpockets stagger into the dark clearing of the cabin. He dropped the dead animal to the earth beside the wood pile. He had to grab the corner logs of the porch to pull himself up the step. Highpockets staggered through the dark doorway and pulled the door closed. He felt his way in the blackness. He bounced off the hard table in the center of the dark room as he groped for the bed. He sat down heavily on a pile of blankets. He tossed his fur hat into the darkness and heaved his legs up to the bed where he lay panting in his fur parka, leggings and boots.

As a chill wind blew down the chimney, the old man drifted into fitful sleep in the cold silence.

Chapter Eighteen

THE WEIGHT OF a mule sat upon the old man's chest as he struggled to fill his lungs with air and with daylight.

Yellow dawn rolled through the windows of the cold cabin as Highpockets coughed inside his parka. He sucked air with an aching chest. He could not breathe.

Lying atop the narrow bed, Highpockets cried out toward the high ceiling. But no sound left his dry mouth, wide open and panting. His white hair was matted with perspiration which ran down his bearded cheeks making tiny, dirty rivulets in the deep creases of his neck.

Highpockets could not move. His mind wandered inside a hazy world of ancient faces and long-gone voices. His stupor was visited by fitful apparitions of companions white and red whose bones were bleached long ago by many summers.

The procession of faces and voices continued as the old man prayed for the terrible weight to lift from his chest. He lived in his feverish mind.

He walked again across a sandbar where low dunes supported two bruised and swollen faces buried to their bloodied chins. A lean, powerful, mountain man with sacks of books strapped to his broad back made many harrowing climbs into the highlands over many summers. The old man watched from afar through his fever. A small, black-eyed child trembled at the end of an old man's musket by a flickering fire on the high plains.

A warrior, ram-rod straight, with painted face and eagle pinions in his long hair, glared at him from his tall mount across a snowy draw. The dark man called out into the thin and freezing air. Highpockets answered in kind.

Crumbled into a small heap on the forest floor, an Indian boy lay bleeding from a roundball which had crashed into his chest below his chin. The ball entered a small, finger-sized hole and then plowed through the boy's naked back leaving behind a wound the size of a man's fist. The dying youth lay at the feet of a tall, very young trapper who stood above him with his hot Hawken rifle in his hands. Onto the white man's furry boots, the child spat black blood. The chilling scream from the young brave called Painted Elk filled the valley where the dead boy lay by the mountain man who had set the child's antlered headdress in his rifle sights. The mountain man, hardly out of his twenties, squinted toward the wail of Painted Elk as the boy's soul took flight with the red-winged hawks of the high places. Painted Elk from afar looked skyward as he felt the grandfathers calling for his son, his only son.

Highpockets shivered on his bed which reeked of sweat and three days of the old man's water. Like that dead boy from a lifetime ago, he coughed dark blood upon his face, flaccid and gaunt from dehydration and fever.

With dawn on the fourth day, Highpockets stirred from his stupor. The weight had departed his thin chest. For an hour, he lay on the soaked blankets and summoned his strength.

Weak from hunger, thirst, and fever, Highpockets stumbled on trembling legs to the floor. Hunched over with weariness and deep pain in his chest, he took small, old-man steps. Then he knelt before the hearth where all of his strength was required to kindle a fire with flint and steel. When a wisp of smoke made for the stone chimney, Highpockets rocked back on his heels and closed his eyes to rest.

Kneeling before the new fire, he reached for the cold coffee pot sitting inside the hearth. He raised the pot to his cracked lips. The cold and bitter coffee made four days ago trickled into his fluttering innards. Coffee oozed down his chin from the corner of his mouth.

Highpockets rose and the cracking of his knees filled the cabin. He peeled the wet and stinking parka from his body, white and shriveled. As the fur dropped to the floor, he shuffled to the larder beside the fireplace. He found a handful of black, jerked venison which chewed hard but went down warm and soothing. Wrapping himself in a long blanket of many colors, he opened the cabin door.

On the front porch, Highpockets had to raise his hand to shield his sore eyes from the ferocious, spring sun. He walked through the woods toward his secret hot springs. He arrived by noon at the steaming bath deep within the trees. He cried softly with relief as the hot, salty water rolled over his body in the cool air.

For two hours he floated without weight in the hot brine. He sucked up the wet heat through one nerve at a time. By mid-day when he hauled himself out of the sublime comfort of the hot pool, the old man was nearly Highpockets of My Mountain. He could straighten his back although his chest still hurt and his head ached. But he felt much relieved.

He wrapped his warm body in the heavy blanket and pulled on his boots. The warm sun took the early spring chill from the air and he was still comfortable when he reached the cabin. The sun just touched the western ridgeline.

Inside the cabin, he renewed the fire before stepping into fresh buckskin trousers and blouse. He ate jerky and hot coffee before he pulled the blackened blankets from his bed. He added his clothing to the blankets and stuffed the pile into a deep kettle at the hearth. Into the iron kettle he added buckets of snow and slush and brown water from puddles drawn from a dozen trips to the door. With the kettle full of his sick cloths and snowmelt, he set the caldron on the fire. Soon thick steam climbed the chimney.

With the cabin tended to, Highpockets went out into the dusk. He rounded the corner and found the hardened carcass of the mulie he had hauled home. He knelt down to lay his whiskered face close to the dried and shriveled deer still in its brown hide. Highpockets was relieved that he did not sniff any sign of rot in the cool meat. Skinning and quartering the kill took all of the old man's strength and it was night before he finished. In the chilly darkness, he wrapped the quartered deer in rags. He heaved the hide, hair-side down, up to the porch roof where tomorrow's sun would help to cure the fleshy side.

He closed the door to the darkness and advanced toward the boiling kettle in the fireplace. With a long ramrod, he pulled the blankets and linens from the brown, swirling water. He draped the laundry over the chairs set close to the hearth where the fire could dry them by morning. Winded and exhausted, Highpockets sank into his hard chair beside the table.

He sucked on his pipe by the fire and its tobac tasted sweeter than he had remembered it. He sat there many hours, rising only to stoke the fire. Although the blankets from the bed were all drying by the fire, the canvas mattress stuffed with dried pine needles felt like goose down.

Morning cascaded in through the windows where the old man lay on the stripped bed. Highpockets stirred with a snort and awoke slowly.

The old man yawned and he touched the floor with stiff legs. He ground fresh coffee. The sound of hand-grinding reminded him of the crunching heard in long-gone camps near Vera Cruz and Buena Vista where Yankees ground black beans before fighting Santa Anna. As the coffee boiled and a venison steak sizzled in the hearth, he picked up the dry, hard blankets from the chairbacks and returned the linens to his bed. One colorful blanket he hung on the cabin wall.

Sitting at the table where black coffee steamed beside a blackened steak, Highpockets smiled at his banquet. He smoothed the wrinkles in the fine, white tablecloth under his tinware.

His heart jumped to his throat at the sudden sound of footsteps on the front porch. He rose instantly and grabbed the loaded revolver from the mantle. He knew that the iron carried four live rounds. He thought of its powder-fouled barrel from sitting uncleaned for a week.

With his left hand on the door latch and his right hand filled with the Navy Colt, he opened the heavy door.

Highpockets squinted into the harsh daylight at the thin figure filling the doorway.

Highpockets took a step backward into the shade of the cabin to get a better view of his company. He sized up the intruder as a buckskinned, white man shorter than himself by a head.

"Enter easy," Highpockets said coldly.

Not until the stranger stepped out of the glaring sunlight did the old man lay eyes upon his Sharps breech-loading rifle clutched in the gloved, right hand. Highpockets recognized a .52 caliber, 1848 model carbine packing a 450-grain ball in quick-loading, paper cartridges.

Both men stood inside the snug cabin. Highpockets looked down into the dirty but clean-shaven face of the thin visitor. The stranger raised his stocky rifle waist-high toward Highpockets' Colt revolver.

Highpockets was had; but he would not fire lightly at another white man. The heavy handiron trembled in his weak hand until he lowered the piece to his side.

The stranger steadied his short carbine which touched Highpockets' chest.

When the intruder sniffed the smell of the venison hanging on the air, the old man spoke.

"Coffee is hot, if you lower that iron."

The stranger glared at Highpockets through brown eyes full of fear and hunger.

"Plenty of meat, too," Highpockets continued.

The stranger said nothing as he backed the old man at rifle-point toward the table in the center of the airy cabin. For an instant, the silent intruder's eyes stopped at the lace tablecloth before his eyes met Highpockets' tired eyes.

When the stranger gestured with his Sharps toward the Colt, Highpockets laid his handiron on the table. The Sharps pushed Highpockets a step away from the table.

The stranger picked up the warm tin cup while his other hand held aim at the old man.

"Drink up, young fellow," Highpockets smiled lamely in the menacing silence.

For the blink of an eye, the stranger was bested by the warm coffee and he closed his eyes in relief. That was time enough for Highpockets' left hand to jerk the Sharps' barrel from his chin while his right hand found the Colt on the table. In the time between heartbeats, the old man was holding the front sight of the Sharps at arm's length. Highpockets' right hand held the revolver muzzle to the bottom of the raised tin cup at the stranger's lips.

"Now you just ease up there," Highpockets growled uncivilly. He rested the handiron's muzzle on the stranger's sweating chin. "You just lay that cannon on the table."

The stranger did as he was ordered. His eyes burned up at his captor.

The visitor raised thin fingers toward his head. When he lifted off his furry hat, short brown hair fell over his grimy ears and furrowed brow.

Highpockets blinked. His face contorted in anguish, as if he were seized by the old pain inside his lungs. The stranger looked fearfully at the sudden wildness in the old man's eyes.

Without a word, Highpockets lowered the Colt. His fingers were white on the handiron's grip.

"I'll not be taken easily, old man," the stranger fumed through clenched teeth.

The stranger spoke fiercely with the voice of a woman.

Chapter Nineteen

HIGHPOCKETS STEPPED BACKWARD until he sat down hard on the bed by the wall. The terrified woman stepped closer to the table where her Sharps lay. Highpockets sat stone faced. The old man looked stricken to the heart when he laid his revolver on the bed.

"I'll not be taken easily," she repeated. She knew the ways of mountain men. When mountain men came to call on the Indian nations, the women often packed their private parts with sand: the only way to keep the white men out.

Highpockets looked up into the softly brown eyes and at the woman's hand which gripped the hilt of a long knife sheathed in her belt.

He raised his large hand to rub hard at the pain in his chest. His eyes focused on the shining floor. He wondered if he beheld another apparition born of feverish stupor. Holding his tender side, Highpockets slowly rose from the bed as the woman laid her filthy hand on the Colt atop the table.

"I never took you before with violence," Highpockets whispered hoarsely behind his wild, white beard. His clear, gray eyes sparkled.

The woman blinked and the color left her ruddy face leaving the grime on ashen skin.

"Merciful Lord," the woman breathed softly with her eyes looking at the lace tablecloth by her side. She raised her pale face toward the old man's battered and furrowed cheeks. "My God," she sighed.

"Elizabeth?" Highpockets pleaded.

The woman's eyes swept the immaculate cabin from the wall of books behind her to the crackling hearth to the old man who towered above her.

Her small hand reached for the hardness of the old man's outstretched hands. She shivered when her hands met his.

"Can it be . . . ," she started to speak, stepping toward the tall man.

"I am called Highpockets now," he interrupted before she could speak his city name which no longer fit. "And you are at My Mountain."

The tall man raised his arms and they alighted gently upon the woman's narrow shoulders. They embraced in silence before the fire. When a chill breeze blew, Highpockets gently pushed her away long enough to close the heavy door.

Turning from the doorway, Highpockets pointed to the small table. The woman smiled through her tears which cut streaks in the dirt on her face. They sat facing each other at the table with the hearth at Highpockets' back. Four hands were locked tightly upon the tablecloth.

"You kept the lace?" she smiled.

"Yes. Near on ten years, I guess."

"You have been up here that long?"

"Longer. More like twenty. I brought the tablecloth with me the last time I saw your face." Highpockets smiled wearily. "Hungry?"

"Starving."

The big man rose and went outside to the quartered buck on the front porch. He returned with a thick steak which he laid into a skillet atop the red-hot stones near the fire. Standing by the hearth, he turned to regard the sitting woman who squinted in a shaft of brilliant daylight coming through the windows. Streaks of gray caught the sunlight playing on her hair. But Highpockets did not see the gray any more than he could see the lines at the corners of her mouth and around her hungry eyes.

"You have not changed, Elizabeth. . . . I am old, but you are the same face which I have carried here." His large hand gently touched his sore chest.

"So you are the famous Highpockets? I had no idea. No idea at all."

"I am."

"It is for you that Painted Elk waits?" she spoke calmly as if stating a fact well known to all.

Highpockets nodded beside the hearth.

"And you will soon go to his council." She did not ask a question.

"You know what I shall do. . . . How is it that you know all of this?"

"The nations allow me to pass freely. They think that I have medicine. I visit with the women and the children."

"Still the teacher, are you?"

"Yes," she smiled looking past the old man toward the sizzling steak.

Highpockets removed the meat from the fire together with the hot pot of black coffee. He flopped the venison onto a tin plate and he filled the tin cup.

The old man sat quietly while the woman devoured the feast. When she finished licking her thin fingers, she sat back and reached for his hard hands.

"Why have you come?" Highpockets asked gently.

"It was hardly deliberate. Like I said, the nations let me pass. Been coming and going through their villages a long time now. You did teach me to live off the land. That's what I do. Only this time I got snowed-in when an avalanche closed the high passes six months ago. I was half starved when I saw your smoke. Been tracking for it maybe three weeks. And here I am." The thin woman smiled and squeezed the old man's hands. "I heard you were dead long ago. How was I to know that you were the trapper the nations call Highpockets and the one Painted Elk has been expecting for damn near a lifetime? . . . You're not really going to his council, are you?"

Highpockets released her hands and rose from the table.

"Welcome to My Mountain. All I have is yours. Anything outside?"

When the woman nodded, the tall man started for the door. He gestured toward the empty pegs on the chimney.

"You can hang the Sharps on the mantle."

"Thanks. Where's your Hawken? You called it Old Martha, right?"

"Gone," he shrugged, stepping into the sunshine where he found the woman's pack on the porch.

Highpockets laid her stores in the corner by the hearth where the boy had laid his bundles.

"Highpockets? I smell like a goat."

"One in rut, at that," the old man laughed. His broad smile full of teeth opened in his white beard. The lines in his haggard face creased deeply. He pulled the blanket of many colors from the wall above the bed. He wrapped the blanket twice around the standing woman's shoulders and he draped his great parka over his back like a furry cape.

"Come, Elizabeth."

Together, they walked into the brilliantly clear morning. Side by side in the last of the dirty snow, he led the woman by the hand through the greening trees toward the hidden, hot springs.

"No weapons, Highpockets?"

"No need. We are never alone here."

They walked for an hour and the old man's back was straight and his step was as quick as the young buck dancing in his heart. Warmed by the fierce sun in the purple sky, Highpockets no longer felt the ache in his ribs as he took his strength from the woman walking briskly at his side.

The woman was winded from his pace by the time they came upon the cloud of white steam rising from the gurgling pool. They squinted against the sun which reflected blindingly from the very last of the snow which lay upon the clearing surrounding the pool. The black water shined like a frothy mirror.

"A bath for my lady," Highpockets smiled as he gently unwrapped the bright blanket from her buckskinned shoulders. There was an awkward silence and the woman smiled meekly.

"In my mind, you are as I remember you . . . all of you." His soft words came on clouds of faint steam in the comfortable spring chill.

Highpockets dropped his parka to the moist earth and he removed his worn shirt. The woman laid her small hand on the ragged scars which crossed the tall man's chest.

"The world has not been kind to you," she whispered through misty eyes.

"It has been kind enough," he said firmly.

Laughing like children, they stepped naked into the hot water which boiled about their bare shoulders in the thin air. The sunlit forest was filled with their sighs as the salty water rolled over them and washed away the muddy grit from the woman's face and the hard years from the old man's heart.

Beneath the hot foam, the woman floated in the brine at Highpockets' side. He floated with his back resting against the pool's rocky side. She nestled in the crook of his long, firm arm. He laid his bearded face upon her wet hair. His tears fell with the salt water dripping from his face.

As they floated locked in each other's arms and without words, moccasinned feet stepped silently as cats away from the pool and away from the private communion of the bathers, so long lost and now found in the sanctuary of My Mountain against the violet sky.

Warmed, rested, and revived, they walked in silence toward the cabin. The woman was wrapped in her long blanket, Highpockets' arm around her shoulders. By the time they reached the cabin, the setting sun cast long shadows across the clearing.

"You go ahead," the woman said. "I'll be in the woods a minute longer."

Highpockets smiled and with an armload of firewood he entered the cabin. He knelt before the hearth until a good fire warmed the chimney stones. Rising, he stroked his wild beard and he stepped to a wooden trunk at the foot of the bed.

From the old trunk, Highpockets pulled a small mirror. He grimaced at the Neanderthal face in the looking glass. He reached for a little leather case deep in the trunk. Rising, he set a kettle of water inside the fireplace before he peeled off his tattered clothing to don fresh trousers and a clean, linen shirt.

Highpockets opened the front door to look for the woman. He saw only muddy footprints and he smiled at the thought of her squatting among the pines.

Returning to the hearth, he wrapped his handkerchief about the hot, iron handle of the boiling kettle. He set the kettle on the table beside the mirror and the leather case. From the case, he pulled a rusted straight razor, a whetstone soaked with whale oil, and a brown chunk of fatty soap melted into the bottom of a shaving mug.

After stropping the blade on the sharpening stone until it shined, he filled the mug with boiling water. With a badger-hair brush, he stirred a thick lather in the mug. Highpockets lathered his beard with the scalding foul-smelling soap.

Then he painfully scraped the years of graying beard from his face one biting stroke at a time with the aged razor. When he had finished, his face was bare, white, and raw. He smiled at the new face in the fogged mirror.

By the time the woman opened the cabin door, Highpockets sat in his chair by the large fire. Blue smoke from his pipe rose to the high, gabled ceiling. The woman blinked at the bare-faced man behind the pipe. Highpockets laid the pipe on the tablecloth and he rose to great her.

Standing before the woman who wore the long blanket around her shoulders, Highpockets was no longer old. The bright fireplace highlighted the deep furrows in his leathery brow and around his smiling, gray eyes. But his clean face glowed soft and white where the razor had carved away the years. The woman raised her hand to the big man's face. Highpockets smiled and he kissed her fingers on his chin.

He pulled her close and they embraced by the fire. When the woman released him, he laid two thick, venison steaks into the hearth skillet.

They ate the meat and they sipped the bitter coffee in the evening twilight. Their laughter and their easy talk and the snapping of the fire filled the cabin with cozy warmth.

When the woman cleared the small table, Highpockets rekindled his pipe. She joined him at the table before the fireplace which made the old man's clean face glow. With one hand, Highpockets nursed his pipe and with the other he held the woman's hand. They spoke with their eyes, his gray and shining, hers warm and brown. Words were too frail to fill the many years between them. So they said nothing which is the way of mountain men—a way the woman had learned long ago from a lean, young trapper of the high places.

Highpockets was in no hurry to take the woman to his lonesome bed. He had no need to end the passions of anticipation. He wished only to sit quietly in her company. The fire crackled and the moon outside cast its glow upon the colorful blankets spread across the narrow bed.

Chapter Twenty

THE WOMAN STIRRED in the old man's arms awakening Highpockets to the sunlight pouring in through the east windows. He tightened his grasp around her shoulders. In the sunlight falling on her hair, she was as young and as smooth as she had been inside the big man's mind. There his most precious treasures were so safely hidden that even Highpockets rarely visited. He feared that a casual opening of the locked door would suffer the hardness of the years to fade the fragile tapestry of an old man's memories: the faces forever fresh, the voices forever happy, and the warm bodies forever hard. But with the woman dozing in his arms and with her head upon his chest, Highpockets was young and supple again.

They dressed by the fire which filled the cabin with a radiance to match the return of love to My Mountain. Were the rising sun in the window to burn black, the cabin would still be warm in the fierce light which was free at last from the narrow hardness of the old man's great heart.

During the days which followed, the pair awoke in each other's arms before leaving the cabin for the greening brush of the mountainside. They walked arm-in-arm in search of new green and the new birds and wildlife which were slowly returning to their high, spring roosts. Their boots made a well worn trail to the hot springs as the sun slowly beat back the last of winter. The days grew longer and the earth claimed the last of the snow to feed the rivulets which thawed and flowed faster and deeper each day.

In the cabin, the sterile order of the old man's world gave way to the touch of the woman who spoke of the wild flowers soon to dress their happy table. At the hearth, the woman worked miracles with the venison and the dried herbs and spices she exhumed from the cabin's crannies and little boxes. At evening twilight while Highpockets took his pipe by the fire, buttons grew on his long woolies and frayed blouses. When the woman discovered a bolt of yellow linen buried in the trunk by their bed, bright curtains appeared on the cabin's windows.

At each day's end, the woman would sit cross-legged on their bed and she would silently watch the old man puff his evening pipe. With Highpockets to do the man's work at the chopping block and water buckets, the woman's hands softened and this added to the illusion of her youth. When she dozed in his arms after his sleepy "Good night, Elizabeth," Highpockets would hold her. He would think about his new vigor which she had found in the ashes.

For a month, they marked the return of the red-winged hawks to the tall Englemann spruces packed densely atop My Mountain. The woman never inquired about the trapper's past. His many ragged scars told that story. Only once did she ask about the occasional, new battle lance which morning would find impaled in the mud close to the cabin.

"It means," the old man said soberly, "that summer has come to the high country."

She held him tightly and turned her face away.

"And it means that we are never alone and that we are well guarded and safe."

She never inquired about the wall of books.

The clearing around the cabin showed more green and less mud. Only the surrounding high peaks held their snow caps. As the air warmed, Highpockets became more restless. His few words became fewer and his mind wandered in the middle of a thought as other burdens creased his clean-shaven face.

When the dream of the woman's comfort had fired the old man's soul for six weeks, she was not the least surprised when he spoke softly through his pipe smoke at their table.

"It is time, Elizabeth."

The glowing cabin was silent while she collected her wits from among the aching pieces of her heart.

"Yes," she whispered before rising from the table for their bed. After tapping out his pipe and stoking the fire, the old man held her tightly. The cabin was dark except for the high ceiling rafters which caught the flickering fire light.

"You are in my heart, Elizabeth. . . . As you have always been."

"And you in mine," she breathed into his white-haired chest.

"Good night, Elizabeth," he sighed as if for the last time in his life.

Morning came too quickly and filled the cabin with clammy grayness from the overcast sky. They dressed slowly in the stillness taking care to memorize their final intimacy.

Over hot coffee, Highpockets spoke first.

"Where will you go?"

"Back among the nations, I suppose. The young braves will be away foraging. The womenfolk will welcome me."

"You will be welcome, indeed. I have packed your things. There is plenty of jerky and coffee. I have no paper cartridges for the Sharps, but I put in a pound of black powder for you to trade down below."

"I will do well, Highpockets."

"I know that for a fact."

"And you will soon go to the lodges of Painted Elk, won't you?"

"Elizabeth, I would sooner that you not go to Painted Elk's camp this season."

Highpockets studied her face. It grieved him to think of her standing at his bleached bones staked to the ground.

"I shall not do that," she whispered.

"You can take the tablecloth with you, if you like."

"No, Highpockets. . . . It can wait here for us."

Highpockets looked away.

An hour later, they stood in the dreary morning a few paces from the cabin. The woman's back was toward the old man and she looked through wet eyes at the distant, blue ridges and a month-long trek to the lowlands.

"You keep to the narrows, now. Follow the stream beds. When they become white water, you will know your way to the nations."

She turned to Highpockets. She was stooped by the heavy sack of stores across her back and the Sharps breech-loader in her arms.

"Oh, Highpockets," she whimpered.

"You will do well."

"Aye, that," she said hoarsely.

Highpockets squinted down at her face twisted with pain.

"Remember the high places," he said firmly with a crooked smile.

Before she might cry out, she turned abruptly and made muddy tracks into the trees.

The woman with tears on her face and chin had not yet reached the dense fir stand as the old man entered the cabin. He closed the door tightly. He could not endure again watching the mountain consume the loves of his life.

Chapter Twenty-One

FOR TWO SLEEPLESS days, the old man busied himself packing his gear. He stuffed his deep sack with the last of the venison freshly dried over the hot hearth stones. The sack bulged with black powder, flints, blankets, and a change of woolies.

At dusk of the second day alone, Highpockets pulled his chair closer to the fire where a small, iron kettle bubbled with molten lead over white-hot embers. Between his buckskinned knees, he set a large barrel of cold water pulled from a new stream of meltwater by the wood pile.

He lifted the bubbling lead closer to the edge of the hearth. With a small, dipping ladle, he scooped up half a cup of melted lead. Carefully, he allowed one silvery drop of liquid metal to drip from the ladle. The searing droplet fell hissing into the water bucket between his legs. Years of experience measured out the precise amount of lead and by the time it sank to the bottom of the barrel, the drop was a perfectly round, lead ball sized to fit the six chambers of the Colt handiron. When all of the melted lead had settled to the bottom, Highpockets recovered two dozen bullets.

He spread the warm roundballs on the bare tabletop. He had already folded the tablecloth and had laid it gently into the trunk by the bed. At the table, Highpockets used an iron file to swage off any excess lead from the bullets. Each ball was slightly larger than the opening of the revolver's chambers. When rammed into the powdered chamber, the overly snug

119

fit would scrape off a fine, white ring of lead at the chamber opening. This tight fit would seal the loaded chambers to prevent a lethal "chain fire" of one ignited chamber setting off another chamber. He dropped the bullets into his possibles pouch.

Before laying the leather bag of tobac into his sack, he filled the pipe with sweet, black Virginia for his nighttime smoke.

Highpockets savoured the pipe as the hearth's fire filled the tidy cabin with many shadows. In the red embers under the fire were the shaving mug and the old razor and the badger-hair shaving brush. The shadows danced on the walls and the ceiling of the log home which he had carved from his forest—the forest which for half a lifetime had sheltered him, clothed him, warmed him, and fed him.

The pipe in his teeth went out with a wet gurgle. Highpockets took the pipe from the new growth of white beard on his face and tapped the pipe empty on the warm stones of the hearth. Standing by the fireplace, he studied the wall of books. He thought of his decision to leave his treasure of gold leaf in the elegant volumes. He nodded to himself. Only some stranger who would be moved to open a book would find the treasure. Such a body would be worthy of such riches, he thought: A man of books becomes what he reads.

After piling new logs into the fire, Highpockets stripped to his long woolies. His old joints cracked as he laid down on the bed. He was exhausted from his sleepless days of bringing perfect order to the cabin.

His mind wandered through the years and it stopped at the familiar faces. He thought about his coming descent from My Mountain to the lodge of Painted Elk and the justice of his council. He felt no fear and when sleep finally came, he slept peacefully and deeply.

With the dawn, Highpockets took his pipe from the mantle and put it into the deep sack which he laid outside the open door. Then he carefully swept the cabin's wood floor until the shine came up. It was not his way to leave a dirty house. His mother had raised him better than that.

Standing on the front porch in the chilly morning, he shouldered his wares and slipped the loaded Colt into his belt. Then he closed the cabin door. On the bare table he left one tin plate beside a tin cup, all to make the next occupant welcome.

Highpockets did not look back when he walked into the forest.

For the first week of his descent from My Mountain, only the red-winged hawks were his company. With each passing day, My Mountain became smaller and its green became more blue. By the second week, My Mountain was lost in the haze.

All of the ice and snow was gone from the mountains. Streams surged with white water and Highpockets slipped on the wet rocks which had been buried by frozen streams when he and the boy had last crossed.

The summer sun brought beads of sweat to his wind-burned face and its three-week beard. The black revolver banged against his thigh until his leg was rubbed raw.

By the fifth week, he emerged from the forest path into the unbroken brightness of the plateau which had been a bleakly frozen tundra when he had last seen it. Now the plain was green and was a sea of blooming wild flowers. Half a day across the field surrounded by distant peaks, Highpockets dropped his sack to the soft earth and he fell to the wet ground to rest.

He lay for an hour, resting his face on his buckskinned arms. The sun was hot on the back of his neck. He dozed all afternoon until the sun approached the western ridges.

When he rose to pitch camp and to kindle his evening fire, he tasted fear when he saw distant plumes of smoke

from other camps far to the north. He squinted to the south
where he saw other fires in the gathering darkness.

The smoke was miles away. He reached into the sack and
pulled out twigs of kindling which he had collected before
leaving the forest for the treeless plain. With the tinder nestled into a small pit dug in the soggy soil, the old man made
a fire to beat back the darkness. He paid no mind to his fire
being seen for twenty miles in all directions.

With his pipe warm in his mouth, he sent his own smoke
to the brilliant stars. The pipe tasted like home and the little
fire soothed his exhausted bones.

Highpockets knew that Painted Elk's braves would keep
the wolf packs from his bed in the tall grass. So he slept
easily.

When morning awoke him, the trapper felt fully revived.
He squinted toward the horizon for Indian sign. Against gray
skies, he saw no smoke.

Warmed by the jerky and hot coffee, he set out across the
plain. He lighted his pipe and puffed as he walked.

He marched all day and nightfall surrounded him with
distant campfires. He slept soundly till the morning. By mid-
day, the warm sun dried his buckskins from their nighttime
dampness. Ground fog gave the illusion of walking knee-
deep in cloud.

Another three days he trekked westward across the wide
savannah. By evening of the fifth day since leaving the
eastern forests, Highpockets made camp at the edge of the
forest which winds down toward the high plains. He gathered his evening kindling from the nearby trees.

Smoking his pipe beside a good fire, Highpockets wrapped
a colorful blanket around his shoulders. He studied the flow-
ered plain and saw a single fire, close.

Highpockets awoke slowly at the forest's edge. He had to
shield his eyes from the low sun in a clear, eastern sky. Stand-

ing beside his warm blankets, he squinted toward the forest fifty paces distant.

Where the trees touched the grassy plateau, a dozen horsemen formed a half-circle between the white man's fire and the trees.

Twelve young riders wore their hair long and braided. Over their shoulders were blankets of many colors. Highpockets did not reach for the black Colt. Although the braves carried bows and knives, not one of the dark-faced youths had set an arrow to his bow. No weapon was drawn.

Chapter Twenty-Two

"YOU ARE THE one called Highpockets," said the leader of the small party. He spoke in the tongue of Painted Elk's people. The old man nodded.

Standing in the dawn sunshine with the horsemen reining in their restless mounts at the forest's edge, Highpockets felt a peculiar relief. The long wait, the restless nights, the days haunted by war lances in the snow, all were ended now. He need fear no more the eyes following his every move from the cover of the forest.

The lead rider who had spoken held the reins of a riderless pony. He dismounted and let his horse chew the moist grass at his shoeless hooves. The leader led the extra pony to Highpockets who still stood beside his pile of blankets and the black Colt handiron lying near the cold firepit. The leader stopped at the white man whose wind-burned face towered above the young brave. The youth handed the reins to Highpockets who nodded.

"Thank ye, kindly," the white man smiled as he mounted the animal. Highpockets' long legs hung low over the girth place of the bare-backed pony.

The painted youth retrieved the old man's sack which he handed up to another painted rider. As Highpockets waited quietly atop his mount, the leader bent down for the revolver. He studied the handiron and its caps pressed upon the weapon's six, loaded chambers.

Walking to Highpockets, the youth silently handed the revolver up to the white man who slipped the weapon into his belt. Such was the old man's integrity known to all with whom he shared the green, high places.

The leader jumped upon his pony's back. After adjusting the longbow slung across his buckskin back, he walked his mount into the forest. Highpockets kicked his pony forward to follow and the other youths fell into single file behind their prisoner. The eastern sky was orange. The western sky was still blue-black.

Highpockets lightly held the reins in his left hand and his right arm lay limply at his side as they rode slowly into the clammy gloom of the thick forest. The soft carpet of the mucky ground muffled the sloshing hooves. They were still high enough in the mountains for the thin air to dissipate the sound of the panting animals.

The white man looked over his furclad shoulder and he counted eleven braves behind him. Each had a single yellow stripe painted across his face. Their young faces were grim and dirty.

The leader steered his pony between the trees over wet ground sloping downward. Highpockets could feel his mount warm and wet against his legs which ached from the strain of keeping his seat over the rugged treescape.

After an hour without words, the pony's smooth gait and the forest's peace overcame the white man. He relaxed his grip on the reins and his pony's head dropped closer to the earth. Highpockets folded his hands on the animal's withers. Confident that his sweating pony would follow the swishing tail just ahead, Highpockets closed his eyes.

The old man opened his eyes when he lurched forward down a steep hill. He picked up the reins and leaned backward as his mount skidded down the hill on his fetlocks. Highpockets could hear the other animals snorting behind him.

From the slick hillside, the leader pulled his pony to one side and the others followed into a dense fir stand. So closely

did the trees grow that when Highpockets looked over his
shoulder he could see only two riders. Within the tree stand,
the leader stopped at a small pond filled with smooth meltwater. Highpockets and the leader dismounted before the
other warriors emerged from the forest.

When the thin leader sat down on a tree stump, Highpockets
rested on a fallen timber wet with moss. They rested for half
an hour before returning to their single-file train between the
trees. They pressed onward all day, resting every two hours.

A full day's ride into the forest, they came to a wide
clearing where the sun burst through the western tree line at
eye-level to the mounted riders. The lead youth reined his
dripping pony to a stop and the little band did likewise. The
young braves and Highpockets secured their horses to a
rope tied to a pair of sturdy evergreens. The men rested
around a blazing firepit. The leader kept his place beside
the white man.

Highpockets sat wrapped in the great blanket from his
sack. He turned to the youth at his side, the leader.

"Why have you come, old man?" the youth demanded in
his native tongue.

"I have come to honor the justice of Painted Elk's council,"
the white man shrugged inside his blanket of many colors
which touched the earth behind him.

"That does not make sense," the youth protested wearily.

"Then why did you wait for me for so long?"

"We came to take you, not to wait for you."

"Oh? To take me? Did Painted Elk send you to *take* me?"
The old man challenged with a squinting glare.

"No," the youth answered softly.

By daybreak on the second day of Highpockets' captivity, the riders were already mounted for an hour and were
making their way between the trees.

They rode in silence during a long and dreary day. Ground
fog was clinging to the steep slopes. They rode carefully to
prevent losing a rider down a slick gorge.

*   *   *

For ten days they meandered their steep course down the rugged mountains. Towering barren peaks and cliffs demanded that the party lead their mounts by hand, single-file for hours.

Through the grueling days, the white man often wondered where the lodges of Painted Elk might be pitched for spring hunting. The nations moved their encampments as the game moved. Highpockets estimated that the summer deer were perhaps two weeks further down the mountains.

After another week, they saw smoke from many fires rising above a wall of trees half a day distant. The sight of home quickened the pace of the young riders.

The leader said nothing when Highpockets kicked his pony onward until he road beside the youth with the painted face. When the young warrior turned to face Highpockets, the old man saw sadness on his gritty face. The leader was half an hour from riding to the lodges of his elders. Within his grasp was his prisoner whose strong medicine had lived in the high places before the youth had been born. But the young man felt no pride. For the old man had come of his own, perverse free will and in his own good time. The leader rode at the side of his captive whom he did not have to capture.

Highpockets still packed his primed handiron in his belt. The leader looked uneasily at the white man. When the youth's face met the resignation which fairly glowed about the white legend's haggard face, the leader stopped his pony. The party stopped behind the two riders. So suddenly did the leader stop that the other braves nearly rode between him and Highpockets. They stopped so close to the encampment that they could smell the burning pine logs in the lodges.

The youth studied the white man's bearded face. The dark faced leader was stricken by the old man's grim dignity which the youth longed to share. He would have traded one of his eagle feathers for an ounce of Highpockets' simple grandeur.

The warrior wanted the old man to break for the safety
of the surrounding forest. He felt for Highpockets' aged
grace just as the white man had felt for the last old deer he
had destroyed atop My Mountain two months earlier. For
many minutes they faced each other while they reined their
pawing animals. Each rider longed to know the other's heart,
but there was no time.

As the sounds of the village children running toward
them filled the air, Highpockets pulled the loaded Colt from
his belt. He laid the iron into the youth's palm.

When Highpockets rode slowly ahead into the sea of
dark children, the youth allowed the old man to ride alone
into the village. It was the leader's silent tribute to the old
white man and to the terrible law of the high places by which
both lived.

Chapter Twenty-Three

THE OLD MAN rested alone for several hours until nightfall. He could hear the noise of the village. Inside his small lodge where he sat beside a fire, thick hide walls muffled the sounds outside.

Hundreds of families rumbled with a rising chatter of anticipation. When the throng became suddenly silent, Highpockets imagined the crowd parting just as the people had divided half a day earlier when the mounted white man rode in alone. Above the fire which burned in a firepit dug in the lodge's earthen floor, a smoke hole in the ceiling opened to brilliant stars. The old man sat cross-legged with his hard hands resting on his buckskinned knees. Here he had been escorted by a round, ancient woman called She Who Laughs. She had black whiskers on her chin. The woman had ushered him inside with courtesy and left him with bowls of roasted meat and warm broth.

As the crowd shuffled quietly, Highpockets rose and faced the sealed doorway of animal skins. The fire highlighted the furrows carved in his face. In the shadows, his face looked like the country in which he lived.

The bearskin opening filled with a wide figure who stepped gracefully into the lodge. The flap closed silently behind him.

With the fire blazing between the two men, Highpockets instantly knew that he faced the chieftain Painted Elk.

Although the white man had never seen this face closer than from across the gorge which had separated them last year in the dead of winter, there was not a moment's doubt. The grand bearing of the bronzed man clad head to moccasin in white buckskin spoke for itself. The chief filled the lodge with himself.

The gravity of worlds radiated from each tall figure. Each measured the other's grim dignity. Each was sovereign in his own place and they faced each other as kings might meet.

The fire sparkled in the white man's clear gray eyes, locked upon black, almond-shaped eyes. Highpockets was struck by the age of Painted Elk. The white man and Cub had looked with snow-blind eyes at Painted Elk. Highpockets had imagined the red man much younger, harder, and thinner. But in the comfortable fire's light, Painted Elk was old—older even than Highpockets.

Painted Elk's wide face was magnificent in the pale light. On it were written seventy winters which had burned its cheeks and all of the summer hunts which had creased it. The furrows and scars on his face reflected the blood on the tall grass in many battles won in his youth making war against other nations. The battles he would no longer fight in the long tomorrow shone in the weariness around his black eyes. In Painted Elk's broad frown was the resolve of old bones determined to climb again the far blue mountains if making meat for the people required another long trail of deer sign in blinding snow.

During his long life among the nations of the high country, Highpockets had seen other faces like this one. But not one of them wore the grave tranquility of Painted Elk who stood an arm's length away.

When Painted Elk gestured toward the floor's pile of blankets, both men sat cross-legged with the fire between them. The midnight chill seeped up from the ground and Highpockets pulled one of the bright blankets around his shoulders. Painted Elk tucked the corners of his grand, fur cape into his lap. The old American with the long braids and eagle feather behind his left ear spoke first with a deeply resonant voice, speaking in the language of the grandfathers which the white man understood.

"Welcome to the lodges of my kind."

The white man nodded and squinted across the fire.

"I, Painted Elk, have waited for you for a lifetime. My council did not believe that you would come after our last meeting in my mountains. But I knew that you would come as surely as the green leaves and the white water come with the long days."

Again, Highpockets nodded.

"My brothers, burning with the passions of youth, wanted to take your hair. But we are too old for that, you and I.

"You are here for the justice of my council. Until the Spirit of the high places moves upon us, you shall be an honored guest. My meat and drink shall be yours. If the Spirit bids you stay, then stay you shall forever; and if the Spirit bids you leave, then you shall go in peace for all your days. That is the word of Painted Elk."

Painted Elk, the law giver, had finished. Outside, it was still dead quiet.

"I have come, Painted Elk, for the justice of your council and of the grandfathers. To share your blankets to keep the chill from my bones will be my honor. I shall wait for the law-giver's council. That is the word of Highpockets."

Rising with one smooth push of his powerful, old legs, Painted Elk waited for the white man who labored to his feet with stiff joints cracking from the long ride down the mountain. Above the fire, Painted Elk spoke slowly.

"You shall not be alone here. This was never my way but the unmanly ways of the young men." The chief paused and sighed the sigh of kings. His dark face softened. "Only the Great Spirit controls all things. But I am only a chief."

When Painted Elk swept out of the lodge, he left the white man blinking at the doorflap which swayed closed.

Before Highpockets would make sense of the chief's words, the flap opened.

For a instant, Highpockets could see the many faces illuminated outside by countless fires and moonlight. Then the short, round form of She Who Laughs passed through the doorway. She dragged a small body by the hand. The child pulled away from the woman and dove into Highpockets before he had time to lift his arms.

"Highpockets! Highpockets!" the terrified child cried, burying his wet face in the big man's chest.

"Cub," the old man breathed as he stroked the boy's hair and looked past him at the woman leaving the lodge.

The trembling boy wept mightily in the old man's firm hug. Highpockets gripped both of the child's shoulders and pushed him to arm's length beside the fire. The old man knelt to face the boy, eye to eye.

"Easy, Cub. Easy now," Highpockets whispered. "I am here."

Highpockets laid his hands on either side of the small, wet face which exploded with a torrent of Russian and Yiddish sobs.

"English, Cub. English," the old man protested gently.

When the boy choked down the last of his tears, Highpockets wrapped a bright blanket around the narrow shoulders. Cub sat down and spoke his English marked by a peculiar lilt of old world accents and mountain drawl. Highpockets smiled at the pleasure of feeling again the boy's melodious speech upon his ears.

The boy spoke into the fire. He talked of his month at the side of Montana Pete as they descended My Mountain. When they camped many months ago on the great plateau of wild flowers, a party of young warriors fell on them. The hostiles all had a single streak of yellow paint on their faces.

Montana Pete and the boy were led to the camp where Highpockets now sat. Two months ago, Pete was taken out, not to be seen again. Cub was delivered to She Who Laughs, the village's Old Mother of the orphans and of those whom the Great Spirit had made children forever.

When Cub finished his tale, he was exhausted. His head dropped to his chest and he leaned against the old man who grieved silently for Montana Pete.

"Here, Cub," said the old man as he gently pushed the boy down to a pile of blankets. He covered him with a red blanket. The boy's eyes were already closed.

Highpockets sat beside the sleeping child. Living more than half a lifetime at the ferocious mercy of the wild places had taught the old man that his life is a puzzle with many pieces which fit together, guided by hands unseen. Looking down at the sleeping boy, Highpockets saw Cub as another brush stroke on the grim canvas of his last days—a portrait which would have had a sorely empty place had the child not slept beside him.

Laying down beside Cub in the snug, firelit lodge, the old man covered himself with one of the blankets. As the fire flickered, Highpockets lay on his aching back and gazed upward through the smokehole toward the sky. Beneath his blanket, the hard earth moved atom by atom until the chilly planet molded herself to fit perfectly the raw bones of his spine. In the stillness, sleep alighted gently on Highpockets' gaunt face. The night breeze carried him aloft to a warm country where unmolested he could dwell among his treasures.

Chapter Twenty-Four

HIGHPOCKETS DID NOT see Painted Elk for another week.

Cub never left Highpockets' side. Although their captivity was absolute, they enjoyed free passage throughout the large encampment. They were free to come and go during daylight which was always bright and cool.

Twice daily, She Who Laughs brought the prisoners their meals of hot meat and coarse bread, washed down by sweet, warm broth. A gritty gruel prepared daily by the fat woman restored the old man's vigor. The aged woman seem pleased when the tall white man would nod and say in her own language, "Thank you, Mother."

Village children, with their herd of scruffy dogs, spent hours at the heels of Highpockets to study their first white man. He welcomed their laughing curiosity and he spoke often with them. The white boy kept his distance from his captors, large or small.

Not until the tenth night of Highpockets' captivity did the doorflap to the lodge swing open and fill with Painted Elk.

The law giver sat down quickly beside the little fire in the center of the floor.

"We are grateful, Law Giver, for the comfort and for the food."

Painted Elk nodded.

"I wish to speak freely," the white man continued. The boy watched closely from a shadowy corner of the lodge. "What became of the white man who came with boy?"

"He was much trouble, this white man," Painted Elk frowned.

Highpockets raised his hand to cover the grin which parted his wild beard.

"Much trouble. My young men wanted to kill him. But that is not my way. So I commanded the council to take the white man's cloths and his weapons and to turn him loose naked and alone in the forest. If the Spirit of the mountains gives him strength, then he shall live. And if not . . ." Painted Elk shrugged and he laid his fists down on his crossed legs. The judgment of the law giver was swift and final.

In the silence, Highpockets wondered if even he could survive alone and naked in the wilderness. The two men watched the fire for a long time. Then Painted Elk rose and waited for the white man to stand before him.

"Tomorrow," the law giver said, "you face the council for the death long ago of my son—my only son." The dark man nearly choked on his last word. "A man's son is his arrow into the future. He has no other. And I have none at all. For this, you will face the council and the grandfathers who dwell in the sky."

For an instant, Painted Elk glared fiercely at the white man. Then his face softened.

"Highpockets," Painted Elk used the white man's name among the nations for the first time, "we are old men, now. We have seen many summers. Together, in our own places, we have enjoyed the lodges of our friends whose spirits now fly with the red-winged hawks. One by one, they have gone away until we alone are left to await our flight away." He looked into the clear, gray eyes of the tall white man close enough to touch. "We should have been friends, you and I."

Without another word, Painted Elk suddenly raised his arms, reaching forward above the small fire toward Highpockets. Immediately, the white man grasped the forearms of the law giver. In the darkened corner, the boy who had not understood their foreign speech sat wide-eyed.

Painted Elk turned sharply and was outside before Highpockets had lowered his arms. The old man sat down near the fire which he fed with kindling piled beside the hide wall. The boy joined him and they watched the fire until the old man spoke calmly.

"It is tomorrow, Cub. I shall face the council for the crime of my youth. You will be safe enough."

The boy had no other inkling of why Highpockets was there, and least of all, why he had planned all winter to come.

"Crime, Highpockets?"

"Cub, long ago and far away, I took a life which was not mine to take." Highpockets spoke into the fire. He thought for a moment about all the lives he had dispatched on the scaffold when he had worn the terrible weight of the long black robe in another world.

"I do not understand," the boy protested.

Highpockets only shrugged toward the fire.

"Ours is not always to understand, Cub."

To the old man's surprise, Cub nodded. The child knew this. He might have been listening to his father's voice. The boy was of Abraham's line, and the eternal struggle to pierce the Veil was his birthright. His people were born to shake their fists at heaven without ever denying heaven. With a mountain man's patience, he could wait.

"Let us sleep, laddy."

With the fire between them and the doorway, they lay side by side. Each covered himself with a blanket of many colors. Their bodies cast a low shadow on the hide wall. The shadows formed a wavy line like the purple ridges visible afar from the crest of My Mountain. Thinking of the distant mountainscape and of My Mountain green against a violet sky, Highpockets was soon there.

Chapter Twenty-Five

DAYLIGHT STAYED OUTSIDE and Cub awoke slowly in the chilly gloom. He rolled over onto his back and reached for the old man.

When he felt only Highpockets' blanket, he bolted to his feet, stumbling over the pile of blankets.

Brilliant sunlight splashed painfully into his face when he ran from the lodge directly into the warm roundness of She Who Laughs. She stopped him in his tracks.

"Highpockets! Highpockets!" the boy cried into the old woman's coarse skirt. He struggled to free himself from her firm grip.

She Who Laughs stroked the sides of the boy's face to calm him. When a gaggle of village children surrounded them, she shooed them away. The boy became still when the heavyset woman laid her hand gently over his mouth. She nodded as if she understood.

The woman escorted the boy by the hand to the village's grassy center which was surrounded by lodges. Between the hide structures were wooden racks for drying fresh, animal skins. The boy walked briskly to a large, circular lodge, larger than any of the others.

The pair stopped and faced four, dour faced youths, each wearing a single streak of yellow paint on his face. The warriors cradled smooth-bore muskets in their arms. Looking skyward, Cub saw a single plume of smoke rising from the center of the great lodge ceiling.

She Who Laughs spoke quickly with one of the painted guards. He then disappeared for many minutes into the lodge. When he returned, he exchanged words with the large woman. She then lowered her face to the boy. The deep, sun-dried creases in her face could not hide the softness of her black eyes. She cared for the boy and he returned a weak smile. When she gestured toward the tentflap of the lodge, the boy took a step toward the guard. When the woman raised a finger to her lips, the boy crept inside the doorway.

Inside, the boy stood in the company of dozens of men all standing with their backs touching the circumference of the lodge. He squinted into the dim light cast by one low fire in the center. Close to the flames Painted Elk sat and the old chief's stony face did not change when Cub looked hard at him. Opposite the fire, Highpockets sat looking across the firepit toward Painted Elk. The boy sighed when he saw that Highpockets still lived.

When Highpockets nodded, the boy stepped sideways until he could elbow his way between two bronzed men whose backs touched the hide walls.

Taking his place, Cub could see that every face faintly lighted by the little fire was old and as cracked as the sun-baked pathways between the village dwellings. He knew that he stood within Painted Elk's council. Only the grandfathers in heaven of this people spoke with more authority than the ancient assembly around him.

The whispering din which had greeted the boy subsided. As his eyes adjusted to the gloom, Cub could make out battle lances propped against the walls. He recognized them as the lances he had seen often in the snows atop My Mountain. He sniffed a faintly sweet odor in the thick air. As the smell filled his lungs, he suddenly had to plant his feet wide on the soft floor to keep his balance. The sickly scent carried the deep voice of Painted Elk.

"My brothers, you are my council, and I, Painted Elk, complete your circle. With us sit the spirits of the grandfathers. With us sit our heirs who are yet to be. And within us is the living breath of our mother, the Earth.

"I am the law giver of this nation. It is our law which this white man had broken so long ago. And it is for our justice which he has come here—of his own free will."

Painted Elk paused and the congregation nodded silently. The boy tried to concentrate on the hard, shrivelled faces all around him. But his head seemed to swim in a gathering haze and the voice of Painted Elk came to him as upon a thick fog. He blinked to summon his senses which were slowly abandoning him.

"It is the spirit of my loins," continued Painted Elk where he sat by the fire, "which this white man has destroyed. When my heart is cold and when my bones are bare to the wind, no one shall come after me. Because of this man, I am the mighty tree whose roots run deep but which shall bring forth neither leaf nor seed. My seasons are for nothing. When my spirit soars away with the red-winged hawks, there shall be an empty hole in the sky." With that, Painted Elk raised both of his wrinkled fists toward the overhead smokehole and his arms made a circle above his head before his hands fell back upon his crossed legs.

A low murmur rolled over the council and the boy could taste the tension in the air as all of the old, dry eyes glared at Highpockets. Cub shifted his weight on legs which felt far away.

A black-faced man stirred near the boy at the rear of the lodge. The company leaned to one side to make room for the old man to pass toward the fire. The man stopped at the side of Highpockets. The painted man was stooped with age and he was thin as a sapling. Toward Highpockets he raised a bony finger and his raspy voice cracked like dry leaves.

"Brothers, this one has taken a life without claim of right. This one has taken a life from our circle, not in battle and not for honor. This one has let loose a spirit before its time and he must pay with his life: also not in battle and not with honor. He should fall like the dog so his spirit will walk only the dark places forever."

When the old man finished, a loud rumble of many voices filled the lodge. Although the boy understood none of the words heard through the haze in his mind, he shivered at the terrible sounds around him.

Painted Elk raised his hand and the clamor stopped. He turned his weathered face to Highpockets who faced him.

"Speak," Painted Elk demanded dryly.

For a full minute, Highpockets did not move nor did he take his gray eyes from Painted Elk's face. When Highpockets stood, he commanded all eyes.

Highpockets stood beside the little fire. The white man looked through the crowd directly toward Cub. Highpockets' square face was as sad as the boy had ever seen it, sadder even than at their parting months ago. Cub's heart fell when he read the resignation which glowed from Highpockets' serene eyes. The boy held his breath as Highpockets gathered his.

"In the high places where my spirit dwells," Highpockets said slowly and softly, "long ago, I took a life which was not mine to take. It was against my will." He paused and sighed deeply. "It was against my will and I have grieved every day since. But it was done."

When Highpockets sat down, Cub was stricken as by a physical blow. He was dumbstruck with disappointment. Although he did not understand any of the white man's words in Painted Elk's language, he could feel the inadequacy of Highpockets' plea. A stillness hung over the assembly. All eyes studied Highpockets who sat by the fire. Like the swooning boy at the back of the lodge, everyone had expected fire to come from the white man's mouth.

Even Painted Elk looked at Highpockets. When Painted Elk heaved himself to his feet, the council was hushed. All eyes were upon him, except for Highpockets' who stared blankly at the dying fire. The chief's brow was creased and the law giver appeared lost in his own thoughts. He looked at Highpockets sitting at his feet and then his eyes swept over the assembly. For the blink of an eye, Cub felt Painted Elk's black eyes stop at his own before moving on. Without a word, Painted Elk pointed toward the tentflap which one of the dark men opened to the blinding daylight outside.

Highpockets rose slowly and walked through the crowd. Cub followed him into the sunshine. The young braves outside pulled the lodge door shut behind the white man and the boy.

Standing in the sun, the boy's head spun and he raised a hand to shield his eyes. His legs were wobbly. Through the throbbing in his head, Cub saw She Who Laughs emerge from a shelter close to the council lodge. She led them toward their own shelter where the three found a fresh fire ablaze on the ground under the smokehole.

Highpockets and the boy sat down. In their momentary silence, the heavy woman left and returned with bowls of hot soup. She looked first at Highpockets and she returned his nod. But she did not smile at the boy as she usually did. Her face was dark with care. She retreated and left them alone with their gruel.

Cub and Highpockets ate silently. The boy was very hungry, perhaps from the bittersweet vapors of the lodge which still pounded in his head. By the time they finished their mid-day meal, the sun was low in the west and their lodge was cool and comfortable.

Laying their wooden bowls aside, Cub watched Highpockets rise and walk to the back of their shelter. From a pile of blankets, the old man found his pipe and the pouch of tobac from his sack. It pleased Cub to sniff the sweet smoke swirling above Highpockets' head when he lit up beside the fire.

"What did you tell them, Highpockets?"

"Tell them, Cub? I told them the truth . . . the God's truth."

"I don't understand, Highpockets."

The boy could not conceal his anger.

"Laddy, I told them guilty as charged," the old man said impatiently upon a cloud of sweet smoke.

"How could you!" The boy was completely out of patience with the quiet mountain man.

"How could I not?" Highpockets spoke softly.

Cub could say nothing to this. He knew better than to attempt to argue with the old man.

"Cub," the tall man offered after a long silence, "the way of Painted Elk is hard. But it is also fair. For as long as the grass has grown, his kind have lived here and learned from the wild places. The law giver will do justly. I am certain of that."

Cub knew when the old man had made a clean exit from a thought. So there would be no more talk this afternoon.

The sky was darkening above the ceiling smokehole when the doorflap opened to make way for Painted Elk. He stood with the firepit between himself and Highpockets who rose stiffly. The boy stayed seated in a gloomy corner.

"It is done," Painted Elk said very gravely in his own language.

Painted Elk looked past Highpockets toward the boy, half-hidden in the shadows. Cub could see only Highpockets' back when Painted Elk raised his long arm and pointed to the boy with the wide eyes and pounding heart.

"The council will have the boy," Painted Elk sighed with anguish written upon his dark and furrowed face. "It was not my way."

Chapter Twenty-Six

HIGHPOCKETS STOOD WITH his mouth open as Painted Elk quickly turned and bowed through the doorflap into the twilight.

"What did he say?" Cub pleaded at the big man's side.

When Highpockets looked down, his wasted face bore a pain which the boy had not seen there before. The battered face made Cub feel sick. The old man knelt on both knees to bring his face closer to the boy's eyes.

"Cub, the council will have blood after all."

Cub was not surprised. He had expected as much after the old man's pitiful speech to the elders. But he was surprised at Highpockets' sudden show of emotion for a judgment which Highpockets had almost demanded.

"Perhaps if you spoke to them again, Highpockets?"

"Maybe," the old man mumbled, turning his face away.

Highpockets shuffled to a pile of twigs and small logs. He laid an armload into the firepit. When the old man knelt beside the fire to work the tinder, it was the first time the boy heard the trapper cursing softly to himself.

As Highpockets poked the fire with a stick, Cub laid a hand upon the old man's shoulder. He felt the muscles tighten.

"Tomorrow, Highpockets, demand to speak again to the council. Ask the old woman."

"Sure. Tomorrow."

By the time the fire was sending good smoke through the smokehole, the sky overhead was black and overcast suggesting a chilly dampness. The fire crackled brightly by the time She Who Laughs entered with bowls of dinner. Cub listened when she spoke unintelligibly to the white man.

"The law giver grieves for thee, old man."

Highpockets looked up from where he sat beside his fire. He studied the black and ancient eyes. Highpockets nodded.

"The council spoke as one voice. The law giver could do nothing." Her voice trailed off with a sigh.

"Old woman," Highpockets said softly, "have you children?"

"Many," the round woman beamed. "All now fly with the red-winged hawk." The fire highlighted the silver in her hair tied severely at the back of her head.

"Then you know," the white man sighed.

The woman bowed her head. When She Who Laughs left the lodge, Cub noticed that she failed to leave him with her cheery goodnight wave.

The two prisoners ate in silence beside the fire. Outside, a hundred fires were kindled to keep out the nighttime cold.

"Tomorrow, Cub, I shall talk with the elders again."

The boy smiled. It pleased him to see that the old man had finally gathered his wits as they chewed sourdough biscuits wrapped around mysterious meat.

"Now we sleep," Highpockets added.

In the warmth of the fire, Cub wrapped a heavy blanket around himself. He soon slept soundly beside the fine fire. Highpockets fired his pipe and sat with his back resting against the sturdy wall of hide.

With his pipe warm in his hand, Highpockets rested his white head against the soft wall. In the quiet of the sleeping village, he savored the pipe and he thought about the council's terrible judgment. The elders' peculiar justice intrigued him. The council had chosen to inflict upon him the precise pain which the white man a lifetime ago had inflicted upon

Painted Elk. Highpockets had expected to die; but the council had reckoned otherwise. And their justice was simple and perfect. He glanced toward the boy who did not know that his days were now few.

It pained Highpockets to think of speaking again to the council. For he could hardly return to plead for justice. Justice had already been meted out, exquisitely. In the high places of the earth, there is no mercy. Of those tested there, only bleached bones or victors remain. There is no middle ground.

All night Highpockets sat there and all night he wrestled with his soul like Jacob with the angel. He was puffing his pipe when the sky above the smokehole turned pink.

With the overcast dawn came the barking of the dogs and the stirring of the village. Highpockets rose stiffly to his feet and added fresh logs to the fire. On the way to stow his pipe in his sack, he nudged the sleeping boy with his foot.

"Morning, Cub."

"Morning, Highpockets."

She Who Laughs soon appeared at the doorway. She carried bowls of gruel and biscuits. She paused to listen to the boy's strange song in which he thanked the God of his father's house for bringing him safely to another day.

"Tell her, Highpockets," Cub demanded. "Tell her."

Highpockets and the old woman made words together which Cub could not understand. Then she left.

"Well?" the boy inquired.

"We shall see, Cub. Now eat up."

They sat beside the fire and ate in silence. It was midmorning when the doorflap opened and a dark-faced man entered. He was a new face, dark and middle-aged. He wore buckskins and across his chest was a fine breastplate formed from white sticks or bones sewn together. His hair was long, black, and braided. He was certainly somebody, the boy thought.

To the boy's surprise, the new man spoke perfect English. The red man reeked of pompous affectation. He stood with his bare shoulders pulled back and his chest strained against his prickly ornaments. His square, hairless chin thrust forward and he spoke to the sky.

"At the Hudspeth Cutoff, near the Humboldt River Trail, I learned the white man's words. I am called Reed Gatherer."

The big man spoke clearly. His hand cut through the warm air of the lodge and he took great pleasure in the sound of his own voice.

"With my mouth, the boy will speak to the council of the law giver. Come." With that, the speaker took long strides to the doorflap.

Cub and Highpockets started for the doorway. Reed Gatherer raised his hand with the grace of a dancer.

"Old man," Reed Gatherer said, "you will wait here. The boy will come alone."

Before Highpockets could protest, Reed Gatherer had gone outside. Cub paused in the doorway.

"It will be alright, Highpockets," the boy smiled. "I shall speak for you to the council. My father taught me well." His eyes shined as he followed Reed Gatherer into the gray morning.

When Highpockets followed, two young braves stopped him at the lodge doorway. "You stay," they commanded.

Highpockets retreated into the lodge where he paced the blankets from wall to wall. He pounded his right fist into his left palm and he cursed the sky for the justice at hand.

Reed Gatherer and the boy arrived side by side at the four warriors guarding the great lodge of Painted Elk's council. The guards moved aside and Reed Gatherer ushered the boy inside. Cub sniffed the bittersweet scent again and he waited for his eyes to focus in the dim shadows. He stumbled behind Reed Gatherer who led him through the throng toward Painted Elk who sat beside the fire in the center.

Foreign words spilled from Reed Gatherer toward the stone face of the law giver. Cub could make nothing of the red man's speech or sweeping gestures. Painted Elk nodded and raised a hand to his face to wipe away the wetness of Reed Gatherer's eloquence. Cub followed Reed Gatherer's lead and sat on the hard ground. All three sat facing the assembly: Cub, Painted Elk, and the Gatherer of Reeds. With his eyes newly accustomed to the gloom, Cub saw that the congregation of elders was sitting. Reed Gatherer turned to the boy and spoke in English which he greatly enjoyed.

"Boy, the council has demanded blood for blood, life for life. Speak now, and by my tongue you shall have the ear of the law giver."

The strange smell hanging in the stuffy air filled Cub's lungs until his head ached. He blinked at the grim faced elders glaring back at him. He turned toward Reed Gatherer who nodded with exaggerated courtesy.

"I have come to speak for my friend who waits for me," the boy said in a firm, clear voice.

Gesturing toward Cub, Reed Gatherer translated, requiring many words to convey the boy's simple remarks.

"I do not know what crime Highpockets committed. But I do know that he is not an evil man. Any crime of his could not have been a crime of the heart."

The Gatherer of Reeds puffed out his chest and covered the assembly with his words. The boy felt the elders shrug at his efforts. When he glanced at Painted Elk, the old chief turned his face away. The boy rubbed his temples which throbbed in the sea of sickly sweet vapors where his mind was wading very slowly, like swimming through syrup.

"Reed Gatherer," the boy said, speaking directly to his interpreter, "tell them that nothing can bring back the life they say Highpockets took. Tell them that the elders of my father's house also have a high court like this council. We call it the Bet Din. Tell them that the Bet Din can also demand death. But when it does, its judges go to their graves branded forever— forever!—as hanging judges. Tell them that, Reed Gatherer!"

The big man sat silently after the boy's rage had filled the chamber. Although the elders could not make out any of the boy's words, they did lean forward in anticipation of the Reed Gatherer's translation of Cub's passion. But the red man waited. He looked over toward Painted Elk who nodded permission for Reed Gatherer to repeat the boy's words.

The Reed Gatherer spoke slowly. He began each sentence in his own language with "The boy says. . . ." When the assembly began to squirm, Cub knew that Reed Gatherer had conveyed his message. When even Painted Elk turned to glare at him, Cub nodded his thanks to Reed Gatherer whose face was impassive.

The uneasiness of the assembly became a rising murmur. When Painted Elk raised his hand, the grave rumblings stopped instantly.

"Reed Gatherer: Tell them that the wise men of my father's people teach that God began the human race with but one human being. That way, all people would understand that to kill one man is like killing all men—as it would have been had the first man died."

As Reed Gatherer spoke, Cub blinked hard to clear the haze from his mind. But the lodge shimmered before his eyes. The shrivelled faces of the elders lit by fire light seemed to rise and fall like a wave of ancient masks. The boy felt sick.

"Tell them, Reed Gatherer, that they have heard my words. I have no more."

The boy's eyes were closed when he finished. He barely heard Reed Gatherer's words.

Painted Elk rose smoothly and said nothing when he pointed toward the doorflap. Cub walked slowly into the daylight. He walked on rubbery legs and stumbled often. Ancient and bony hands steadied him until he staggered through the doorflap into the soft arms of She Who Laughs.

Together, the boy and the old woman walked arm-in-arm through the village. She pushed the boy into Highpockets' lodge where he found the old man standing beside the fire-pit. The woman stayed outside.

"Highpockets," the boy sighed.

"I am here, Cub," the big man smiled as he wrapped his arms around the boy.

"I told them, Highpockets. I used all my words. They were not many," Cub shrugged. "I did my very best."

"Yes, laddy. Of course you did." The old man wiped a tear from Cub's face.

They sat down together beside the fire. Highpockets handed the boy a bowl of water which he sipped dry. When he had finished, Cub looked into Highpockets' kind face.

"What if I failed?"

The old man said nothing. He reached behind the boy and pulled a blanket around Cub's shoulders.

"Rest, Cub."

The boy curled up inside the thick blanket and laid his head next to Highpockets.

"I did my best," Cub whispered.

Highpockets was silent as he stroked the boy's black hair. The old man raised his face toward the smokehole and the close gray sky.

Chapter Twenty-Seven

THE PALE SUN was low in the west when Cub stirred after a three-hour nap. Highpockets sat nearby with a blanket wrapped around his broad shoulders.

"Is it late?" Cub muttered, wiping his eyes.

"Nearly dark." He handed the boy a wooden bowl of broth which the old woman had brought while the boy slept. It was spring and with the new green came many new babies. She Who Laughs hovered over the toddlers so their mothers could nurse infants. When she had entered the prisoners' lodge earlier, she had stroked the forehead of the sleeping boy. He was just one more of her little ones.

"Was their news while I slept?" Cub asked, sitting up and sipping from the wooden bowl.

Highpockets nodded and looked into the fire.

"And? And?" the boy urged. He was fully revived by the sleep and the soup.

"I shall live, boy." The old man choked on his words.

"Oh Highpockets!" Cub shouted. He threw his arms around the big man's shoulders.

Highpockets pushed the boy down until they sat side-by-side.

"Cub," Highpockets began as he stood up, "the council has spoken. You must walk-about. It is the way of the law giver." The standing man turned his back to the sitting boy.

"What is this walk-about?"

"The council has decided to send you into the forest half a moon distant. You will go alone and unarmed. They will take you into the mountains and leave you there." The tall man winced at his own words. "No food. No weapon. No water. . . . Nothing." Highpockets spoke to the closed doorflap. "You will have fourteen days to find your way back to this village."

"And if I can return in two weeks?"

"Then together we shall leave this place in peace."

"And if I cannot get back in time?" the boy's throat was suddenly very dry. He reached for the bowl of broth.

Highpockets could not bring his lips to say, "Then only I shall leave here." So he shrugged. He lifted the boy bodily until he stood close to the tall man's buckskinned chest.

"Cub, listen to me. You will leave tomorrow at dawn. Mark my words." The old man's words came out hard as stone in an icy voice which the boy had not heard since they had first met with a rifle barrel between them.

"Cub, I do not want you to return here. You are not to come back. Do you understand me?" Highpockets squeezed the boy's arms so hard that it hurt.

"Highpockets, I do not understand. I must come back. For you. . . . For you."

The old man could not tell Cub that it was not Highpockets' life which the council wanted. The trapper feared for the boy's safety if he returned. Painted Elk had the power to spare Cub's life, but only if the law giver lived and only if his medicine continued to have authority. Highpockets did not trust the younger men who had humiliated and perhaps had killed Montana Pete. Highpockets' heart ached as it had not ached since the woman of his youth had disappeared into the forest of My Mountain. He summoned all of his strength to face the fearful child. His voice was colder and harder than the winter ice atop My Mountain.

"Cub, I forbid you to come back here. I saved your life once. Now I am telling you what I want in return: You are not to come back here."

Highpockets was nearly raving. The old man's words fell on the boy as if blow by blow from Highpockets' huge fists. When the big man took a step toward the terrified child, Cub stepped backward and raised his hands to protect his face from the crazed man.

Turning his back to the old man, Cub retreated to a dark corner of the lodge. He sat down upon a bright blanket and looked at the hide wall close to his leaking eyes. Highpockets watched his trembling back.

"Tomorrow I shall go, Highpockets."

"Yes," the old man whispered from his broken heart.

Highpockets' shuddering sigh filled the lodge when She Who Laughs entered. She stood in the firelight which glistened in the white man's gray eyes. She understood the care in his worn-out face.

"My heart is with thee," she said softly.

The old man nodded and she went outside into the darkness. Highpockets looked at the fire for an hour. He and the boy sat back to back. Cub did not look up when Reed Gatherer entered.

"I bring food and drink for the boy to give him strength for tomorrow." Reed Gatherer laid two wooden bowls at the boy's feet. "You must eat, boy." Reed Gatherer laid a third bowl beside Highpockets. "You too, old man," he harumphed. "It is the will of the law giver."

Reed Gatherer departed. Highpockets did not look at the bowl of food. In a corner of the lodge, Cub ate quietly.

After another hour of silence, Highpockets stood and wrapped his shoulders inside a blanket. He lowered his head to get through the doorflap which he found to be unguarded. He walked alone through the village toward the lodge of the council of elders. Only one brave stood at the tentflap. At the white man's approach, the youth opened the doorway as if the old man were expected.

Inside the circular lodge, the stale air was black. Highpockets crept through the blackness to the center of the enclosure where his foot stumbled over the edge of the fire-pit. He sat down on a pile of blankets where Painted Elk had sat. In the darkness, Highpockets closed his eyes which changed nothing in the lodge black as death. He listened to his own breathing and he could smell the pine ash in the cold firepit by his crossed legs.

Highpockets opened his eyes when he heard the distant doorflap open. In the doorway he saw Painted Elk standing with a flaming torch in his hands. The law giver entered and approached the sitting white man who looked up from under his gray eyebrows.

Painted Elk lowered the torch into the firepit and smoke rose toward the overhead smokehole. The chief sat down at Highpockets' side. The small fire bathed the lodge in pale light. Neither old man looked at the other. They watched the fire for a long time and when they spoke, their words came softly.

"Your law is hard, Painted Elk. Cruel and hard."

"It is the law of the high places," the dark man said dryly.

"It is not my law," Highpockets sighed.

"Nor is it always mine, my brother. Think not that it was I who demanded the blood of the child. I, I of all my council, know that it is a sin against nature for a father to bury his son."

"That may be, Law Giver. But I could not save the child of Painted Elk. You can save this child before it is too late."

Neither old man looked into the face of the other.

"I am only one voice of many here," the chief continued. "It was I who saved you and the boy from the stake when the sun climbs over the eastern mountains. I could not do more."

Highpockets pulled the blanket closer to his neck in the cold dampness.

"Is not my life enough for you, Law Giver? My hand killed your son so very long ago. I should pay. I should know the justice of Painted Elk."

"You have known my justice. The boy in the forest shall be alone. But by your hand will he live or die, just like my son." Painted Elk faced Highpockets. "How have you taught him?"

Highpockets' mind came back to the law giver's perfect justice.

"I taught him well, Law Giver. His hands are soft. But the boy's heart is as the young lion." The white man nodded toward the fire.

"Then there will be justice: the justice of the high places," Painted Elk said firmly. "The boy must have his father's heart."

Highpockets turned to face the chief.

"Will that be enough?"

"Such is not for us to say." Painted Elk paused to collect his thoughts in the chill darkness. "Our seasons are few now. Our days are only waiting days—waiting for our spirits to fly away. Soon enough, you and I will come to learn all of the mysteries. But now, we must wait. We are become our memories. It is for young men to become their dreams."

Painted Elk saw the white man nod. The fire was slowly failing. Only a small sphere of light touched the weathered faces of the two old men. Painted Elk rose easily to his feet. Highpockets had to place his hands upon the ground to heave himself upward. The law giver turned his face away from the white man's creaking effort to stand. Then Painted Elk faced Highpockets, eyeball to eyeball.

"My brother," the law giver said warmly, "it is my prayer to the grandfathers that one day our spirits shall fly together in the high places of the Earth."

Highpockets looked at the old chief's lined face and into the deeply set, black eyes where the firelight twinkled.

"Yes, Law Giver."

The sky was black and the stars moved between wisps of low cloud when Highpockets walked to his lodge. He found Cub sitting close to the fire in the center. The flames gave the shelter an inappropriate coziness. Highpockets dropped a few twigs into the fire. He spread his blankets on the floor and made his bed as far from the boy as the small lodge would permit.

"You will do well, Cub," Highpockets said stiffly as he climbed into his blankets.

"I will do well," Cub said without taking his eyes from the fire by his knees.

After an hour, Highpockets heard the boy spread his blankets at the far side of the lodge opposite the firepit. Softly, Cub intoned his evening prayers. As he listened, Highpockets could not stop the tear which followed the deep furrow on his cheek.

A bustle at the lodge doorway woke the sleeping prisoners. The doorflap opened and Reed Gatherer filled the entrance. His long arm reached outside into the night. Highpockets and Cub sat up sleepily to watch the red man's grunting effort to pull something inside the lodge.

"Come, bitch!" Reed Gatherer bellowed through the open flap.

The Gatherer of Reeds dragged into the lodge a child with long, black hair. He pulled again until the dark-faced waif stood elbow-high to the big man. In the pale darkness, the boy and Highpockets stared at the child wrapped in a blanket at Reed Gatherer's side.

The Reed Gatherer pulled the frightened child's blanket away to reveal a girl not much older than the boy. She clutched her arms to her small, naked breasts. The boy's eyes opened wide in the firelight.

"For the boy," Reed Gatherer snickered, "that he might know manhood before his walk-about come daybreak." He grinned at the naked child. "A gift from the council." In a moment Reed Gatherer was gone, leaving behind the trembling girl who dropped silent tears onto her bare feet. She was a slave captive from some raiding party to the lowlands.

Highpockets looked at the boy who sat up with his mouth still open.

"Sleep where you wish, laddy," Highpockets said with a smile he could not hide. At least the council does not hand out justice by halves, Highpockets thought. He rolled over toward the hide wall to give Cub what privacy he could.

Cub blinked at the girl. In his sleepy mind, he was struck by a memory not yet one year old. Looking at the slave girl, the sight of another girl dead and maimed beside a rocky creek spilled over him. He shivered in the warm firelight and looked away from the slave who hid her dirty face in her small hands.

When Highpockets heard shuffling feet, he wished that he could sleep elsewhere. He felt Cub snuggle under his blankets. The old man laid out his arm beneath the boy's head. They heard the slave girl climb into the boy's warm blankets. Her soft whimpering filled the lodge.

For a long time, Highpockets and Cub looked up together toward the ceiling. The boy was soon sleeping soundly in the crook of the old man's arm. Highpockets did not sleep. He kept watch over Cub until the first pink appeared overhead in the smokehole.

Chapter Twenty-Eight

THE DISTANT SOUND of drums filled the lodge by the time the boy stirred at the side of Highpockets. Inside the doorflap were wooden bowls of smoked fish, warm broth, and wild berries, deposited before daylight by She Who Laughs. The boy rubbed his eyes and looked at the empty blankets where the girl had lain. She was gone.

Many voices outside joined the drums. The boy's morning prayer chants mingled discordantly with the villagers.

"Come, Cub." Highpockets knew that the law giver's justice would come swiftly. "Soon you will be on your way. You know enough to survive. Keep to the high country where the bear and the bobcat will stay below you. Keep your face into the wind. The forest will provide." Highpockets squinted down into the boy's face. "And mind me: You are not to return here. You are to go west to the lowlands. But you cannot come back up here. It will not be safe for you here."

As the old man turned his tortured face away, Cub's heart sank. His evening prayer had been that Highpockets would forget his admonition not to return.

The doorflap opened and She Who Laughs entered in the company of the Reed Gatherer. The thick woman walked directly to the boy. She laid her hands on his shoulders and looked sadly into his dark eyes.

"May your mother the Earth be kind to thee. Tell my sons who fly among the red-winged hawks that I come soon to soar with them and with the grandfathers." The woman kissed his forehead. Cub smiled although he understood none of her words. Highpockets stood off to the side where he said nothing.

"Come, boy," demanded the Gatherer of Reeds with overbearing gravity.

The old woman turned to look into the face of Highpockets. She said nothing to him but her brooding eyes joined his for a long moment. Then she was gone into the morning daylight.

Highpockets walked toward the boy who waited beside Reed Gatherer. It was difficult for Cub to look up into the white man's anguished face. Highpockets laid his heavy arms on Cub's shoulders. When the two prisoners started for the doorflap, Reed Gatherer stopped them with his thick arm.

"No, old man. Only the boy."

Cub walked manfully from Highpockets' grasp. At Reed Gatherer's side, Cub turned to face Highpockets. But as the boy turned, the old man turned too, and all Cub saw was Highpockets' back. In silence, the boy walked with Reed Gatherer into the fierce daylight.

Inside the lodge, Highpockets sat beside the cold firepit. His eyes were closed and his large hands rested on his knees. The song of the village and the rhythm of the drums poured into his mind. Above the maddening din, Highpockets heard a faraway, red-winged hawk call out his name.

The boy raised his hand against the blinding sun. Two rows of villagers lined the well-trod path running the length of the encampment. The chorus of voices and the many drums filled the boy's head as he walked at Reed Gatherer's side toward the council's lodge.

At the entrance to the great lodge, six mounted horsemen reined in their ponies. The leader held the reins of a riderless horse with a blanket laid across his bony spine. Three of the riders held a lead-rope secured to a loaded pack-horse full of provisions. Reed Gatherer abandoned the boy when the village closed in upon him. Cub searched the crowd for the friendly face of the old woman but he could not see her. Nor could he see Painted Elk. Behind him, a thin plume of smoke rose from the smokehole of the council lodge.

Out of the crowd hobbled the ancient man whom Cub remembered as the frail speaker at the first meeting of the council. The cadaverous man stopped at the boy who looked up into his brown skin stretched tightly across a smooth skull. The crowd became silent but the drums continued like a great heart.

The old man raised his face toward the sky and his rasping voice croaked. He stooped and scooped up a fistful of dry soil. With a groan of effort, he stood erect and let the earth fall slowly from his bony fingers upon the boy's head. Then the village resumed its song and Cub felt a tug at his sleeve. He looked up into the mounted youth's painted face. Cub followed the leader's gesture and mounted the riderless pony.

The multitude broke into two lines on each side of the path which ran from the council lodge to the forest half a mile distant. Cub could taste his heart.

Slowly, the mounted men and their pack animals walked between the swaying, singing villagers. They rode past the lodge where Highpockets sat with his wet eyes closed. Cub looked sideways and shouted. "I shall remember the high places." But his words were lost in the clamor all around him.

When the green forest covered the riders, Cub could hear the village for a long time before the dense firs swallowed up their song. When he finally rode in silence, he closed his eyes and prayed. He prayed that the mountain man would take care to keep the rain and the snow from his precious treasure of ancient books and silver candlesticks which lay in the lap of Highpockets.

*   *   *

Two weeks they rode. In single file, the seven riders and their trailing, draft animals walked through the forest ever downward toward the west.

They rested hourly to preserve the horses. Often they rode carefully at night so the darkness would confuse the white boy's sense of time and place. The council's word had been clear to the war party: Cub's walk-about was to be like a blind man cast adrift in black water.

On the fifteenth day, the little band stopped at noon in a clearing surrounded by trees. They drank their fill of a cool stream where Cub knelt beside the white water. He wore only his tattered trousers and his coarse peasant blouse with its dangling, dirty fringes hanging beneath his shirt tails. He wore his short-billed hat pulled down tightly to keep out the chilly wind. Barefoot, he possessed nothing else: no food, no weapon, no boots, nothing.

After sipping his fill of the cool water, Cub stood to face the six youths waiting behind him with the ponies.

The boy turned but he saw only trees and bare rocks and a gray sky. The tracks of the ponies led to the stream where they disappeared in the clear water.

Beneath heavy clouds, the boy stood alone. He made one slow circle on his heels in the wet grass. He heard in his mind the old man's order to go west. Then he started walking east toward the village half a moon away.

When the night was cold and dark, Cub fashioned a lean-to shelter from tree branches rich with soft pine needles. With the rope holding up his trousers, he made a spring-hole snare which he set along a well-worn, rabbit path. When the forest provided, he ate and had fur to cover his cold ears.

With a narrow strip of pelt from the fruits of his snare, he made a firebow to cook his meager ration and to warm his nights.

Cub spent many hours squatting by a rocky stream where he made a bola with ragged rocks at each end of the last of his belt rope. With it, he stalked a tiny deer. When he brought the buck down, from the white ligaments on either side of the animal's spine he made long threads of sinew. He sewed the animal's hide with the dried sinew to make moccasins when his bare feet left bloody footprints on the pine needles of the forest floor. From sinew threads he also made a fishing snare. With the sinew noose, he snagged fish by their gills along the rivers.

Like the Pah-Ute nation, he nourished himself with the spring, flowering ends of the wild cattails. He treated himself to the sweet ribbons of sap layer beneath the bark of the aspen firs. He dried strips of the fragile layer to carry with him during his climb back along the steep path to the village of his captivity.

He looked around tree stumps for wild partridge berries clinging to their winter vines.

Cub did not reach the encampment for five weeks. Instead of finding the village, he stood among rain-filled firepits in the great clearing. Tall grass grew were the lodges had been.

Where the round lodge of the council had stood, there were many rotting bodies wrapped in bear skins atop funeral alters high in the cool air.

Dressed in his rags, Cub walked among the death towers. He came upon the newer graves in the air. The wind had not yet unwrapped the bodies to reveal moulding flesh to the sun. On one freshly wrapped bearskin shroud, he saw the feathered headdress of Painted Elk, the law giver.

And Cub saw dangling from the law giver's airy tomb a long tail of white hair suspended from skin dry as brown paper. He gently removed the scalp and buried it in the warm, moist earth of the high country.

By the place where the scalp was hung, he found propped against the law giver's high bier a rusting rifle. The shooting iron's browned barrel pointed skyward and it glowed in the burning daylight. Cub had carried that Hawken before.

He did not linger. Cub shouldered Old Martha and turned his back upon the empty campsite and its puddles of rotten water. He retraced his steps down the mountains toward the

west and toward the hard company of white men in clap-
board towns beside the wagon trail.

In his heart, Cub carried the face of the old man he loved.
And he carried in his mind the winding green trail to My
Mountain and the golden treasure waiting there.